Prescription Murder

A Drama in Three Acts

by William Link
and
Richard Levinson

A Samuel French Acting Edition

FOUNDED 1830

New York Hollywood London Toronto
SAMUELFRENCH.COM

Copyright © 1963, Under Title RX MURDER
by William Link and Richard Levinson
Copyright © 1963 by William Link and Richard Levinson

ALL RIGHTS RESERVED

CAUTION: Professionals and amateurs are hereby warned that *PRESCRIPTION: MURDER* is subject to a Licensing Fee. It is fully protected under the copyright laws of the United States of America, the British Commonwealth, including Canada, and all other countries of the Copyright Union. All rights, including professional, amateur, motion picture, recitation, lecturing, public reading, radio broadcasting, television and the rights of translation into foreign languages are strictly reserved. In its present form the play is dedicated to the reading public only.

The amateur live stage performance rights to *PRESCRIPTION: MURDER* are controlled exclusively by Samuel French, Inc., and licensing arrangements and performance licenses must be secured well in advance of presentation. PLEASE NOTE that amateur Licensing Fees are set upon application in accordance with your producing circumstances. When applying for a licensing quotation and a performance license please give us the number of performances intended, dates of production, your seating capacity and admission fee. Licensing Fees are payable one week before the opening performance of the play to Samuel French, Inc., at 45 W. 25th Street, New York, NY 10010.

Licensing Fee of the required amount must be paid whether the play is presented for charity or gain and whether or not admission is charged.

Stock licensing fees quoted upon application to Samuel French, Inc.

For all other rights than those stipulated above, apply to: William Morris Endeavor Entertainment, 1325 Avenue of the Americas, New York, NY 10019

Particular emphasis is laid on the question of amateur or professional readings, permission and terms for which must be secured in writing from Samuel French, Inc.

Copying from this book in whole or in part is strictly forbidden by law, and the right of performance is not transferable.

Whenever the play is produced the following notice must appear on all programs, printing and advertising for the play: "Produced by special arrangement with Samuel French, Inc."

Due authorship credit must be given on all programs, printing and advertising for the play.

No one shall commit or authorize any act or omission by which the copyright of, or the right to copyright, this play may be impaired.

No one shall make any changes in this play for the purpose of production.

Publication of this play does not imply availability for performance. Both amateurs and professionals considering a production are strongly advised in their own interests to apply to Samuel French, Inc., for written permission before starting rehearsals, advertising, or booking a theatre.

No part of this book may be reproduced, stored in a retrieval system, or transmitted in any form, by any means, now known or yet to be invented, including mechanical, electronic, photocopying, recording, videotaping, or otherwise, without the prior written permission of the publisher.

ISBN 978-0-573-61424-8   Printed in U.S.A.   #5124

STORY OF THE PLAY

Dr. Roy Flemming, a brilliant New York psychiatrist, can no longer tolerate his marriage to his neurotic, possessive wife. With the aid of his mistress he evolves an ingenious murder plan that depends on a bizarre impersonation to create a perfect alibi. The scheme is carried out successfully, but the police officer assigned to the case, Lieutenant Columbo, grows suspicious. He is a formidable adversary. Though he seems to be a bumbling, forgetful, almost inept bureaucrat, he is actually a shrewd professional with a deep knowledge of human nature. He and Flemming engage in a cat-and-mouse duel of wits, in which the psychiatrist has to improvise at top speed in order to counter Columbo's sly tactics. He hounds the doctor with annoying questions, drops by his office, and even says with seeming innocence that he'd like to become a patient. Flemming is finally forced to use political influence to have him removed from the case, but this does not stop the tenacious policeman. Realizing that the mistress is the weak link in Flemming's defenses, he subjects the girl to a harsh interrogation and uses her to trap the doctor in a surprising climax.

PRESCRIPTION: MURDER was first presented on the stage by Paul Gregory in association with Amy Lynn at the Curran Theatre, San Francisco, on January 20, 1962. The cast was as follows:

MISS PETRIE	.........................*Lucille Fenton*
DR. ROY FLEMMING	...................*Joseph Cotton*
CLAIRE FLEMMING	.................*Agnes Moorehead*
SUSAN HUDSON	......................*Patricia Medina*
LIEUTENANT COLUMBO	..............*Thomas Mitchell*
DAVE GORDON	......................*Howard Wierum*
DELIVERY BOY	.....................*Raleigh Davidson*

SYNOPSIS OF SCENES

The action of the play takes place in New York City.

ACT ONE

SCENE 1: Dr. Flemming's office. A Friday afternoon in late May.
SCENE 2: The Flemming apartment. That evening.

ACT TWO

SCENE 1: The Flemming apartment. Monday morning.
SCENE 2: Dr. Flemming's office. The following Friday afternoon.
SCENE 3: The Flemming apartment. A half-hour later.

ACT THREE

SCENE 1: Dr. Flemming's office. Late the same afternoon.
SCENE 2: Lieutenant Columbo's office. Later that night.
SCENE 3: Dr. Flemming's office. The following morning.

DESCRIPTION OF CHARACTERS

DR. ROY FLEMMING: A polished, urbane New York psychiatrist in his forties. Highly civilized, pragmatic, at all times gives the impression of a cold, functioning intelligence. He wears conservative, artfully-tailored suits.

CLAIRE FLEMMING: A brittle, sardonic product of New York's East Side. She is in her early forties and shows the strain of a loveless marriage. Her clothes, like her apartment, are ultra chic, and in one scene she wears a negligee.

SUSAN HUDSON: Young and extremely attractive, with a hint of latent sensuality. She is not particularly complicated, but as the play progresses she shows the burden of increasing tension. She dresses with the stylish taste of an actress.

LIEUTENANT COLUMBO: A rumpled police official of indeterminate age. He seems to be bumbling and vague, with an overly apologetic, almost deferential manner. This masks an innate shrewdness, however, a foxy knowledge of human nature. He wears an undistinguished brown suit, an old topcoat, and a battered felt hat throughout the play.

DAVE GORDON: A smooth, boyish lawyer with his eye on a political future. Wears the accepted Ivy League uniform.

MISS PETRIE: A pleasant, efficient woman in her fifties with a genuine liking for people. She wears sensible office attire.

DELIVERY BOY: Early twenties. Either wears nondescript street clothes or a jacket with MADISON CLEANERS lettered on its back.

PRODUCTION NOTE

The two actresses playing CLAIRE FLEMMING and SUSAN HUDSON, though they needn't be strictly similar in face or figure, should have approximately the same hair coloring.

Prescription: Murder

ACT ONE

Scene 1

TIME: *Two P. M. on a Friday in May.*

PLACE: *The reception room and office of* DOCTOR ROY FLEMMING. *The reception room is at Right, a clean-edged, functional area with a desk, several tufted chairs, and a long coffee table dotted with ceramic ash trays and lined with some of the better magazines—"Harpers," "Vogue," "The Saturday Review." There are lamps and two end tables, and nested in each table are waxed green plants. A door at Right leads to a corridor and the elevators. Another door, at Left, connects with the office. The office is large and comfortable, decorated in soft tones of brown and green. There is a bookcase, a desk, and in the center of the room are two facing chairs of the Eero Saarinen variety, deep, starkly modern "potato chip" chairs on metal bases. The bases are locked to the floor, but the seating portions can be revolved in any direction. Standing on the carpet by the desk is a black attaché case.*

AT RISE: *The Stage is dark, and we hear a TELEPHONE ring. The LIGHTS come up to reveal the receptionist,* MISS PETRIE, *a middle-aged woman with a crisp, professional manner. She answers the phone.*

MISS PETRIE. Doctor Flemming's office. . . . Yes, Mrs. Logan. . . . No, the doctor won't be available tomorrow, he'll be out of town. . . . Just a minute, I'll check. (*She opens an appointment book on her desk.*) The first free

8   PRESCRIPTION: MURDER   ACT I

hour is next Tuesday, three to four. . . . Fine, I'll put you down. (*She hangs up and jots something in the appointment book; then she gathers a few papers and enters the doctor's office; she places them on his desk and turns to leave when his PHONE rings; a little annoyed, she answers it.*) Doctor Flemming's office. . . . (*The voice on the other end of the wire increases her annoyance; this is a "problem" patient—she hears from him at least three times a day.*) Oh, hello, Mister Sussman. . . . No, he's out to lunch. . . . Well, he should be back soon. . . . No, I don't know *what* restaurant, there are about six in the neighborhood. . . . I really think if you'd call back in a few minutes. . . . All right, I'll have him call you. . . . Yes, as soon as he comes in. . . . (*While she talks, the door to the corridor opens and* ROY FLEMMING *enters; he is a polished, urbane man of forty, with an easy charm and a quick and resourceful intelligence; his manner is engaging, but there is a certain sharp precision to him, a decisive, almost automatic method of response; he starts toward his office.* MISS PETRIE *looks up as he enters; then, to phone:*) Just a minute, please. . . . (*She cups the mouthpiece.*) Doctor— (*Wryly indicating phone.*) Mister Sussman.

FLEMMING. Oh, God.

MISS PETRIE. Shall I tell him you're busy?

FLEMMING. (*Sighs.*) No, I'll take it. (MISS PETRIE *gives him the receiver.*) Hello, Harry, this is Doctor Flemming. What's the problem? . . . Um-hmmm. . . . Um-hmmm. . . . Well, if you want to go to the track, go to the track. . . . You *don't* want to go to the track. Then don't go, it's that simple. . . . Not at all, Harry. Glad to be of service. (*He hangs up, looks ruefully at* MISS PETRIE.) I wonder if he'll send me a card on Father's Day.

MISS PETRIE. He called this morning, said he was feeling hostile. I didn't know what to tell him.

FLEMMING. Next time prescribe acetate of salicylic acid.

MISS PETRIE. What?

ACT I PRESCRIPTION: MURDER 9

FLEMMING. Aspirin.
MISS PETRIE. (*Smiling.*) I take it Mister Sussman is in the positive transference stage.
FLEMMING. (*Wryly.*) With bells on.

(*She goes into the reception office, closing the door behind her; FLEMMING glances at his watch, then lights a cigarette and exhales thoughtfully; finally, his eyes fall on the attaché case; he picks it up and sets it on the desk, opening it so that its back is toward the audience; for a few moments he rummages around inside, then he removes a folded cloth bundle; he shakes it out and we see that it's a woman's gray wool dress; he studies it reflectively, holding it at arm's length. The door to the reception room opens and CLAIRE FLEMMING enters, wearing sun glasses and carrying a pair of white gloves; she is a woman in her late thirties, very chic, with a tendency toward middle-aged heaviness in her face and arms; on the surface she appears confident, but occasionally she falters, showing a certain emotional instability; she crosses to Miss Petrie's desk.*)

CLAIRE. (*Brightly.*) Hello, Miss Petrie.
MISS PETRIE. Oh, hello, Mrs. Flemming.
CLAIRE. Is he in?
MISS PETRIE. (*Nods.*) I'll buzz him. (*She picks up the phone and rings the office.*)
FLEMMING. (*Drapes the dress over his arm and answers.*) Yes?
MISS PETRIE. Your wife is here, Doctor.
FLEMMING. (*A pause.*) Ask her to come in. (*He hangs up quickly, folds the dress, and begins putting it into his attaché case; while he is doing this:*)
MISS PETRIE. (*Indicating office.*) You know the way.

(CLAIRE *flashes her a smile and crosses to the connecting door; she enters the office just as* FLEMMING *finishes closing the case.*)

CLAIRE. (*Brittle, forced, with a slight sardonic edge.*) Hello, darling. I've been on a shopping safari all morning. Just thought I'd peek in. Busy?

FLEMMING. (*Consults his watch again.*) I will be. I'm expecting a patient.

CLAIRE. I suppose I should have called, but that wouldn't have been spontaneous. I had lunch with Sybil.

FLEMMING. How is she?

CLAIRE. Same as ever. She and Dave are going house hunting this week end. I think it's ridiculous. They don't really need it, and the thought of the two of them rattling around in a reconstructed farmhouse—well, it's out of character. (*Surveys room.*) The place looks nice. When was the last time I was here?

FLEMMING. A month ago.

CLAIRE. That recently? I'd forgotten. (*Goes to bookcase, picks up one lying on top, reads title.*) "My Life in Art," by Stanislavski. Very impressive. Are you treating actors now?

FLEMMING. A few.

CLAIRE. Must be fascinating. They have rather prolific love lives, don't they? And so public. You'll have to tell me about it sometime.

FLEMMING. (*Patiently.*) What can I do for you, Claire?

CLAIRE. (*Deliberately vague.*) Do for me? Nothing. I just dropped by to say hello. You don't mind, do you? I'm only taking a few seconds out of your fifty-minute hour. Besides, I won't be here when your patient comes. I wouldn't want to disturb him—or her.

FLEMMING. (*Quietly.*) All right, Claire, what is it?

CLAIRE. (*Abruptly.*) Yes, I will have a drink, thank you. (*She crosses to the bar and makes herself a drink; then, as if she's just heard him.*) What is what? Really, Roy, you act as if I had some motive for coming over here. I told you. I just dropped by. (*Drink in hand, she walks around the office, aimlessly touching surfaces. He watches her.*) We bumped into a friend of Sybil's at lunch. Silly woman, quite inquisitive. As soon as she found out what you did for a living, she began asking questions.

It appears she's thinking of undergoing analysis. She wanted to know how it felt being married to a psychiatrist. Aren't you interested in what I told her? . . . I said it was like living light years away from Mount Palomar. You know you're being watched, but you can't see the telescope. I'm not sure she understood me. Anyway, that's one of my stock answers. I usually talk about living in a glass house— (*A touch of bitterness.*) living *alone* in a glass house. . . . (*Brightening.*) She had quite a supply of psychiatrist jokes. There was one—but I'm sure you've heard it.

FLEMMING. Claire—we both know you have something to say. When are you going to say it?

CLAIRE. Indulge me, darling. Listening to people is your profession. And you should be available for your own wife. Or is that nepotism?

FLEMMING. I imagine you'll get to the point eventually.

CLAIRE. Oh, yes, this office is built for getting to the point. It's always reminded me of a confessional. And the secrets you must hear— (*Pause.*) I waited up for you last night.

FLEMMING. Did you?

CLAIRE. You didn't get in till three. Where were you?

FLEMMING. Where I said I'd be. With Doctor Cobb.

CLAIRE. Till three in the morning? Bill Cobb's seventy years old. His wife tells me he's usually asleep by ten.

FLEMMING. Last night he wasn't. We were talking about one of his cases at the clinic. We lost track of the time.

CLAIRE. (*A pause; she removes her sun glasses.*) I don't believe you.

FLEMMING. (*Studies her; then, coolly.*) Why should you? I'm lying. I was in bed with my mistress.

CLAIRE. Roy—

FLEMMING. Or if that doesn't suit you—let's see—I had dinner and went to the theatre with a high-priced call girl.

CLAIRE. I just—

FLEMMING. (*Interrupting.*) You said you waited up. Why didn't you talk to me last night? Or this morning?

Isn't the breakfast table the place for this kind of discussion?

CLAIRE. (*Defensively.*) I wanted to think.

FLEMMING. That's the trouble with you, Claire. You think too much. (*Then, in a kinder tone.*) Look, these things have a way of magnifying themselves. You're upset now. Why don't we go into it later when you're feeling calmer?

CLAIRE. (*Flaring.*) Damn it, Roy, don't patronize me. I won't have you treating me like a patient.

FLEMMING. You're acting like one, aren't you? (*He picks up a phone, begins to dial.*)

CLAIRE. (*A touch of fear.*) Who are you calling?

FLEMMING. Bill Cobb. I want you to ask him what time I left his house.

CLAIRE. Oh, fine. What will that prove? He's a friend of yours.

FLEMMING. (*Immediately hangs up and starts dialing another number.*) All right, you can talk to his wife. She's a friend of *yours.*

(*He holds out the phone. Hesitantly,* CLAIRE *takes it; she looks at it for a few beats, not placing it to her ear; then, defeated, she slowly cradles it.*)

CLAIRE. (*Softly.*) I'm sorry—

FLEMMING. (*Goes to her, takes her in his arms; his voice is gentle, as if he's talking to a child.*) Why don't we just forget about it? And the next time something worries you, you'll tell me, won't you? (*She nods.*) People have enough things to bother them without creating problems. (*Kisses her on the forehead.*) Now. Feel better?

CLAIRE. (*Nods again.*) Darling, I know I get bitchy sometimes, but it's only because I'm jealous. I can't help it. Maybe when we're alone, when we can talk things out— That's why this week end is so important to me.

FLEMMING. I know.

CLAIRE. And we'll have a good time, won't we?

FLEMMING. Of course we will.

CLAIRE. We should have done it long ago. It's just what we need. No phone calls, no interruptions—

FLEMMING. (*Smiles, goes along with her.*) Not even the Sunday *Times*.

CLAIRE. I'm actually getting excited.

FLEMMING. Good. Now suppose you go home and pack.

CLAIRE. (*Lightly.*) What makes you think I haven't?

FLEMMING. (*Lightly.*) Because you always put everything off till the last minute.

CLAIRE. Will you be home early?

FLEMMING. I'll try. (*Kisses her on the cheek.*) See you tonight.

(*During this, the reception room door has opened and* SUSAN HUDSON *has come in; she is a brunette in her late twenties with a strong sexual attraction; she seems nervous.*)

MISS PETRIE. Hello, Miss Hudson.
SUSAN. Hello.

(*At this moment,* FLEMMING *opens the door and follows* CLAIRE *into the reception room;* SUSAN *turns and looks at her;* CLAIRE, *oblivious, goes out.*)

FLEMMING. (*Briskly, to* SUSAN.) Good afternoon, Miss Hudson. Won't you come in? (SUSAN *enters the office; she settles herself, not quite comfortably, in one of the "potato chip" chairs;* FLEMMING *comes in and sits in the other; during this,* MISS PETRIE *removes a folder from a file by her desk, enters the office, and hands it to* FLEMMING.) No calls, Miss Petrie.

(*She nods and goes out, closing the door. There is a moment of silence, then* FLEMMING *and* SUSAN *move into each other's arms; they kiss hungrily.*)

SUSAN. Oh, darling, darling, I've missed you!
FLEMMING. And I've missed you.

SUSAN. I almost called you yesterday. Rehearsals broke up early and I went for a walk in the park. It was so lovely. You know that carousel near the bridge? I actually wanted to take a ride. Isn't that foolish?

FLEMMING. Not at all.

SUSAN. I knew you'd be busy. But I could just picture the two of us spinning around like idiots.

FLEMMING. We'll do it sometimes. I'll wear my homburg and we'll pose for vodka ads. (*Kisses her again.*) How's the play?

SUSAN. Everyone's fighting. I think we're changing directors in midstream.

FLEMMING. What about your rehearsal schedule?

SUSAN. I have to go back for a few hours. But then I'm free for the week end.

FLEMMING. Good.

SUSAN. (*Pause.*) That woman who was just here. That was Claire, wasn't it?

FLEMMING. It's called E.S.P.—extrasensory perception. (*Smiles.*) There's a theory it only exists between women. (SUSAN *has been sobered by the thought of Claire, her mood darkens slightly; she digs in her purse for a cigarette and* FLEMMING *lights it.*) You're tense.

SUSAN. A little.

FLEMMING. Did you sleep last night?

SUSAN. No. . . . Well, maybe an hour or two.

FLEMMING. (*Studies her, then crosses to his desk, takes a pad from a drawer, and begins writing on it.*) This is a prescription. Have it filled at the drugstore downstairs.

SUSAN. What is it?

FLEMMING. Sleeping pills. (*He tears off the slip and hands it to her.*)

SUSAN. (*She puts it in her purse, then suddenly turns to him imploringly.*) Roy, can't we wait for a while?

FLEMMING. (*Firmly.*) No.

SUSAN. Just a little more time to think it over.

FLEMMING. How long? A week, a month, a year? Or shall we put it off indefinitely?

SUSAN. I didn't say that. It's just—

FLEMMING. (*Soothingly.*) It's just that you're nervous. And that's very natural. But, darling, face facts—you're going to be nervous whenever we do it.

SUSAN. (*Troubled.*) I keep wishing there were some other way.

FLEMMING. There isn't.

SUSAN. But if you talk to her. If *I* talk to her.

FLEMMING. (*Amused.*) Susan, you're wonderful. Really. But just a bit naive. What do you think Claire would do if you went to her? She'd listen politely—probably even give you a cup of coffee—all very modern and civilized. Then she'd consult with her friends and re-read Norman Vincent Peale for inspiration. Finally, she'd do the exact opposite of what I want—she'd forgive me.

SUSAN. Are you sure?

FLEMMING. Darling, she's a professional martyr. (*Takes her arms.*) Look—a long time ago I decided that my wife and I were incompatible, sexually, intellectually— (*Slight smile.*) and even politically. So I asked her for a divorce. She refused. A year later I asked again. She refused again. She told me, quite clearly, that she intended to live with me for the rest of her life. And she meant it. . . . The Claires of the world don't get divorced. Their daughters do—frequently, but not the Claires.

SUSAN. How can you be so positive?

FLEMMING. Because I've been studying them for a long time, in this room and at home. (*Faintly mocking.*) They're an amazing sisterhood. Every day is the same. They roll out of bed into Bonwits; they have lunch in town with their friends; they have one martini—just one—before dinner. But the remarkable thing is that they're tenacious as hell. Divorce is a dirty word, so even though they may not sleep with a husband, or even talk to him, they won't let him go.

SUSAN. When you talk like that I wonder if you'll ever get tired of me.

FLEMMING. Tired of you? (*Meaning it.*) Darling, I want you to understand something. When a man my age falls in love he commits himself. He doesn't have time for adolescent fixations.

SUSAN. All right, I'm younger than Claire, I'm prettier. But are we really so different? She's probably more intelligent than I am.

FLEMMING. It's a destructive intelligence. She's bitter to the point of being an emotional invalid. Besides, what makes you so sure that intellect is what I need in a woman?

SUSAN. Need? You haven't used that word before.

FLEMMING. An oversight. Easily corrected. (*Holds out his arms.*) Come here. (*They embrace again.*) I need you—

SUSAN. (*Fiercely.*) Roy, I love you. (*Then she moves away.*) If I didn't, I—don't know how I'd go through with this.

FLEMMING. But you will.

SUSAN. Yes.

FLEMMING. (*Suddenly quite businesslike.*) Now— (*He opens the attaché case and removes dress.*) This is the dress. I want you to be sure it will fit.

SUSAN. (*Takes it, examines it, then holds it up against her.*) It might be a little big.

FLEMMING. Enough to be noticeable?

SUSAN. No, I don't think so.

FLEMMING. Are you positive? Do you want to try it on?

SUSAN. It'll be all right. Shall I—take it home with me?

FLEMMING. No. I just brought it so you could check the size. I don't want you wearing it until it's necessary. (*He folds it on the desk and takes a glossy 8 x 10 photograph from the attaché case.*) This is the clearest photograph I have. In the others she's either wearing her sun glasses or standing at a distance. (*Hands it to her.*) Notice her makeup.

SUSAN. She uses a heavy eyebrow pencil.

FLEMMING. And plenty of lipstick. She has a full lower lip so she doesn't cover the lipline. (*He watches her as she studies the picture.*) Take that with you for reference, but be sure to bring it tonight. (*She folds the picture and puts it in her purse.*) Are you clear on the timing?

SUSAN. I'll be at your apartment at ten o'clock.

FLEMMING. But no sooner. How do you get there? Cab?

SUSAN. You're testing me.

FLEMMING. Do you mind?

SUSAN. No, not really. I suppose we both have to be sure of things. I won't take a cab; I'll come by bus. I'll get off a few blocks away and walk.

FLEMMING. Good girl. The apartment number?

SUSAN. Six K. I ring your bell twice.

FLEMMING. Anything else? (*Pause.*) Susan?

SUSAN. The sun glasses.

FLEMMING. Right. And a large purse for the dress. Now are you sure of everything? Do you want me to go over it again?

SUSAN. No. I don't want to think about it any more.

FLEMMING. It's going to be fine, darling. Believe me.

SUSAN. I don't know. . . . None of this seems real.

FLEMMING. But it is. (*Looks at her for a long moment.*) We've thought about it for months. We've walked around the edges, we've backed away, and now it's finally going to happen. After ten o'clock tonight nothing can change it. You understand that?

SUSAN. Yes.

FLEMMING. Then go back to your rehearsal. As soon as you're free, go home and get some sleep. I'll see you tonight. (*They embrace; she clings to him as if she doesn't want to go, then she breaks away and starts for the door.*) Susan— (*She turns, startled;* FLEMMING *crosses to the bookcase and picks up the Stanislavski volume.*) you'd better take this. (*He holds it out. She looks at it uncomprehendingly; he opens the cover and reads the inscription.*) "To Roy: All my love, Susan."

(*Wordlessly, she takes it; he smiles at her encouragingly and she goes out.*)

MISS PETRIE. Good-bye, Miss Hudson.

18 PRESCRIPTION: MURDER ACT I

SUSAN. (*Vague.*) Good-bye. (*She exits.*)

(FLEMMING *rings the outer office.*)

MISS PETRIE. (*Answering.*) Yes, Doctor?
FLEMMING. I'll be going out of town this week end, Miss Petrie. If there are any emergency calls, refer them to Doctor Cobb.
MISS PETRIE. Will you be leaving your address?
FLEMMING. No. My wife and I are taking a little vacation upstate. We don't want to be disturbed.
MISS PETRIE. I hope you enjoy yourselves.
FLEMMING. I'm sure we will. (*Starts to hang up.*)
MISS PETRIE. Doctor—
FLEMMING. Yes?
MISS PETRIE. I just wanted to say that Mrs. Flemming looked very lovely today.
FLEMMING. Thank you. (*He hangs up and folds Claire's dress, putting it back in the attaché case. Then he removes a small tissue-paper package from his jacket pocket. He peels away the tissue, revealing a pair of gloves. Carefully, he tries them on, inching them down over each finger. He is flexing his hands as:*)

THE LIGHTS GO OUT

END OF SCENE 1

ACT ONE

SCENE 2

TIME: *It is 9:45 Friday evening.*

PLACE: *The living room of the Flemmings' apartment in the East Seventies. The living room is large and spacious, ultra-modern. It has a cold, impersonal quality, as if Claire knew her husband would always be a*

ACT I PRESCRIPTION: MURDER 19

guest, never a permanent resident. Long, low furniture, a liquor cabinet, and several contemporary abstracts on the walls. French doors lead to a terrace overlooking the city. A desk stands to one side and next to it a breakfront. Branching off, although we cannot see them, are a dining area and kitchen. At Left is a door to the entrance corridor, and at Right is a door to the bedroom. Flemming's attaché case is on the desk.

AT RISE: *The LIGHTS come up as* CLAIRE *enters from the bedroom, crosses to the phone, and dials a number. She wears a negligee.*

CLAIRE. (*To phone.*) Hello? Syracuse Airlines? . . . Yes, I'll wait. . . . Hello? I'd like some information, please. Is Flight Twelve-A leaving on schedule? . . . Eleven o'clock? Thank you. (*She hangs up, goes to her purse, and removes an emory board. She tries, ungracefully, to buff her nails. Then she calls toward the bedroom.*) Darling?

FLEMMING. (*From bedroom.*) Yes?

CLAIRE. I just called the airline. The plane's taking off on time.

FLEMMING. (*Off.*) Fine. (CLAIRE *sees the attaché case on the desk and crosses to it. She unsnaps the fasteners, starts to open it.* FLEMMING *enters from the bedroom; he is in shirtsleeves and in the process of knotting his tie.*) What are you doing?

CLAIRE. Looking for the tickets.

FLEMMING. They're not in there—I have them in my jacket. You'd better hurry, hadn't you?

CLAIRE. (*Closing the case.*) Now, don't rush me, dear. I hate the feeling of having to rush. Besides, planes never leave when they're supposed to. Remember when you had to go to California for that analytic seminar? I think we sat in that terminal for three hours. It *was* three hours, wasn't it, Roy?

FLEMMING. (*Hardly listening.*) Just about.

CLAIRE. And you were so angry. I'll never forget the look on your face. (*Laughs.*) You were ready to charter a Greyhound bus. (*While she talks,* FLEMMING *tackles the cufflinks in his shirt.*) Here, let me help you. (*She fixes them.*) You're a brilliant man, darling, but you're not very mechanical.

FLEMMING. (*A thin smile.*) That's what wives are for.

CLAIRE. That and everything else. Have you finished packing?

FLEMMING. A few more odds and ends. What about you?

CLAIRE. I fought that battle this afternoon. Oh, by the way, Dave Gordon called.

FLEMMING. Anything important?

CLAIRE. No. Just wishing us a pleasant trip. He and Sybil want to get away next month.

FLEMMING. Nice of him to call. He's busy these days.

CLAIRE. Sybil told me at lunch he's prosecuting two cases next week. I suppose it serves him right for having political ambitions— (*A thought suddenly strikes her.*) Do you think Dave will ever be governor?

FLEMMING. It's possible.

CLAIRE. Sybil in the governor's mansion. Well, it's better than a reconverted farmhouse. . . . Do you remember when Dave was going to law school?

FLEMMING. Vaguely.

CLAIRE. (*Reflectively.*) So many years ago. He was working during the days at that place in the Village, and then classes at night. I don't know where he got the time to study.

FLEMMING. (*Smiles.*) He borrowed it from me, darling. I had plenty to spare.

CLAIRE. (*Affectionately.*) Why didn't you ever burn any midnight oil?

FLEMMING. I didn't have to. My wife had a rich father.

CLAIRE. (*Playing along.*) And you married me for my money.

FLEMMING. Not yours, darling. Your father's.

CLAIRE. (*Reproving, but not really serious.*) Now, Roy, you shouldn't even joke about that.

FLEMMING. Of course I shouldn't. But I'm afraid I'll never be governor.

CLAIRE. You don't have to be. I love you anyway. (*Pause. She holds out her hand.*) And you love me. Don't you, Roy?

FLEMMING. (*Takes the beckoning hand; kisses her mechanically.*) Very much.

CLAIRE. (*Thoughtfully.*) Sometimes I wonder what would have happened if we had children.

FLEMMING. They'd probably be supporting us by now.

CLAIRE. No, I'm serious. Are you ever sorry we didn't have a family?

FLEMMING. I hardly think about it.

CLAIRE. I do. Too much, I suppose. I know I didn't want one in the beginning. There was always your practice, and neither of us seemed to have the time— (*Slight smile.*) and I didn't want to ruin my figure. (*Wryly.*) That's happened anyway, hasn't it?

FLEMMING. Not at all.

CLAIRE. Yes, it has. But you're very flattering, darling.

FLEMMING. (*Looks at his watch.*) Claire—the maid's coming in tomorrow, isn't she?

CLAIRE. As far as I know.

FLEMMING. Give her a call and check, will you? Sometimes she forgets.

CLAIRE. Oh, I don't think she will.

FLEMMING. (*A veiled order.*) Call her, anyway.

CLAIRE. (*Puzzled.*) All right, dear. (*She goes to the phone, lifts the receiver from the hook; then she pauses.*) Roy—did you see my gray wool dress?

FLEMMING. What?

CLAIRE. My wool dress, the gray one. I was going to take it with me but I can't seem to find it.

FLEMMING. Maybe you sent it to the cleaners.

CLAIRE. (*Reflectively.*) No—it should be in the closet. Well— (*She dials a number. While she talks on the phone,* FLEMMING *crosses to his attaché case on the desk, opens it, and removes the gloves. He half-turns away from her and slips them slowly, almost delicately, over his fingers. To phone.*) Hello, Charlotte? . . . Charlotte, this is Mrs. Flemming. I just wanted to make sure you'd be in tomorrow. . . . About ten o'clock? You have your key, don't you? . . . Fine. 'By-by. (*Hangs up.*) She's coming in at ten.

FLEMMING. (*His hands in his pockets.*) Good.

CLAIRE. (*Crossing to the bar. She begins mixing a drink.* FLEMMING *approaches behind her.*) She's a dependable girl. We're lucky to have her. Some of the servants these days are unbelievable. (*Turns with the drink, holds it out.*) Drink, darling?

FLEMMING. (*Caught off guard. He can't reveal his gloved hands.*) Not now. Set it down, will you?

CLAIRE. (*She puts the glass on the bar and crosses to the French doors; she opens them and inhales the air; her negligee billows slightly in the breeze.*) It's such a beautiful night, isn't it?

FLEMMING. I hadn't noticed.

CLAIRE. Perfect flying weather. I can see for miles. You know, I've never been frightened on a plane. I wonder why? Actually, when you come right down to it, you're all sealed up in metal, and if anything goes wrong what are your chances? I suppose it's the same with a car, though. And the way some people drive— (*He has been moving up behind her, until he stands a few inches away; abruptly, she turns.*) Do you know what I've been thinking?

FLEMMING. What?

CLAIRE. When we get back I'm going to redecorate the apartment. It's so cold now—it needs warmer colors. It looks as if no one really lives here. Besides, we haven't had a party in ages. I think we should start entertaining again. Wouldn't it be nice to have people over for a change?

FLEMMING. If you like.

CLAIRE. You'd like it too, wouldn't you? (*Happily.*) And we're going to have such a wonderful time this week end. Did you tell anyone where we're going?

FLEMMING. Miss Petrie knows we'll be upstate, but I haven't told her about the lodge.

CLAIRE. You really love that place. Have you ever taken a woman up there besides me? I mean, before we were married?

FLEMMING. Dozens. Providing they didn't mind digging for worms.

CLAIRE. Well, I'm not outdoorsy, darling, but we'll have a good time, anyway. (*She puts her arms around him in a little hug of affection; he responds, stroking her back with his gloved hands.*) I'll hang my stockings in the bathroom and we'll have a week end of sin.

FLEMMING. You'd better close the window and get dressed.

(*She turns and latches the French doors;* FLEMMING *braces himself.*)

CLAIRE. (*Drawing the curtains aside and looking into the sky.*) Well, a few more hours and we'll be there. A second honeymoon. (*Smiles.*) Might even be better than the first.

(*His hands suddenly shoot around her neck, the fingers closing;* CLAIRE *stiffens with shock and begins to struggle against him; there is a sheen of sweat on his forehead and we hear her gagging, the taut pull of breath in her throat. The TELEPHONE rings.* FLEMMING *looks at it wildly, then frantically increases his pressure; finally he lets go and she slides to the floor; he breathes heavily for a moment, then hurries to the phone and snatches it up.*)

FLEMMING. Hello? . . . Oh—hello, Dave, how are you? . . . Yes, Claire told me you called. . . . Fine, we're just leaving. No, be back Monday. That's right.

. . . Claire? No, she—she's dressing. I'll tell her. Listen, I'd better get going. Give our love to Sybil. (*He hangs up and stands absolutely still, orienting himself; from this point on his actions are careful, cool, and controlled; he goes to the desk and picks up a heavy quartz paperweight; hefting it, he crosses to the French doors, opens them, and steps out on the terrace. After glancing in both directions, he shatters one of the door's glass panels; then he returns to the living room and replaces the paperweight. He pauses, wipes at his forehead with the back of a gloved hand; he disappears into the bedroom for a moment and returns with two suitcases. He opens one of them on the floor and begins removing silverware and valuable knick-knacks from the breakfront. He drops these in the suitcase, adds two silver lighters and an expensive piece of statuary. Then he picks up Claire's purse, stuffs its money in his pocket, and scatters the rest of the contents on the floor. He goes into the bedroom again, comes out a moment later wearing his jacket and carrying Claire's mink wrap, a pair of her gloves, her jewelry box and a bundle of laundry. He drops the armload on the couch just as the DOORBELL rings twice. He checks his watch, then crosses to the door and puts the chain on. He opens it as far as it will go and looks out. Then he unlatches it and* SUSAN *comes in, her face drawn and anxious; her hair is pulled back in Claire's style and her lipstick and eyebrow lines are emphasized; she carries a large handbag. She comes further into the room, sees* CLAIRE'S *body and stops dead; she gives a small, involuntary gasp and brings her hand up to her mouth. Sharply.*) Susan! (*She doesn't seem to hear him; she turns away from the body, trembling. As he closes the door behind her.*) Did anyone see you come up? (*She shakes her head.*) There's a drink on the bar. Take it.

SUSAN. I don't—

FLEMMING. Take it! (*Dumbly, she walks toward the bar. Removing his gloves.*) And wear these.

SUSAN. (*Looks at the gloves, realizes he wore them to*

strangle Claire.) No. Please. I don't need a drink. I'll—I'll be all right.

FLEMMING. Did you get some rest?

SUSAN. Yes.

FLEMMING. No, you didn't.

SUSAN. (*Snapping.*) All right, I didn't. I said I'd be all right.

FLEMMING. (*Examines her critically, then stuffs the gloves in his breast pocket.*) Be careful not to touch anything. Did you bring the photograph? (*She opens her purse and hands him the picture of Claire. He folds it and drops it in the open suitcase.*) You'd better get ready. (*He crosses to his attaché case, opens it, and gives her the dress; she remains motionless.*) Well, put it on.

(*She goes into the bedroom.* FLEMMING *drops the gloves into the open suitcase, adds the mink wrap. Then he opens the jewelry box and spills the contents into a handkerchief.* SUSAN *enters from the bedroom. She is wearing Claire's dress, and though the two women are not alike, there should be a fleeting moment of similarity.* FLEMMING *looks at her approvingly. She stuffs the dress she was wearing into her purse, then notices the jewelry box and opens handkerchief in his palm.*)

SUSAN. (*Apprehensively.*) What are you doing with her jewelry?

FLEMMING. (*Knotting the handkerchief and dropping it in the suitcase.*) There's a lake three miles from the lodge. By tomorrow morning they'll be at the bottom with the rest of these things. (*He closes and fastens the suitcase, stands it and the other one by the door.*)

SUSAN. Are we ready?

FLEMMING. (*Looks at his watch.*) Not yet. Make your call to the cleaners. (*Opens address book.*) Here's the number.

SUSAN. Won't they be closed this time of night?

FLEMMING. They're open till twelve. (*Indicates phone.*) Go ahead.

SUSAN. (*Nervously.*) Can't you?
FLEMMING. If you won't make a simple phone call—

(*She starts for the phone, but before she can pick it up he stops her. He takes a handkerchief from his pocket and wraps it around the receiver; then he dials and hands her the phone.*)

SUSAN. (*Faltering.*) Madison Cleaners? . . . This is— this is Mrs. Flemming, apartment 6-K, 23 East 72nd. I— I have a bundle of laundry and some things to clean—
FLEMMING. (*Whispers.*) It'll be outside the door.
SUSAN. I'm—I'm leaving it outside the door. Will you have someone pick it up the first thing in the morning? Apartment 6-K, yes. Thank you. (*She hangs up, trembling.*)

(*The handkerchief is still wrapped around the receiver; neither she nor* FLEMMING *notices it.*)

FLEMMING. (*Comforting.*) That was fine. We're almost ready. Put on the sun glasses. (*She rummages in her handbag. Impatiently.*) Where are they?
SUSAN. I know I brought them— (*She keeps searching; finally she finds them and puts them on.*)
FLEMMING. Good. (*He hands her the gloves.*) Put these on.
SUSAN. Why?
FLEMMING. She always wore them with that dress. (*As she puts on the gloves, he takes the laundry bundle and opens the hall door.*) When you come back from the airport, add her dress and gloves to this bundle. (*He sets it outside in the corridor, comes in and closes the door.*)
SUSAN. Why couldn't I come in and put them away?
FLEMMING. I don't want you in the apartment, it's too dangerous. Besides, I'd rather have them cleaned so there'll be no trace of your wearing them. (*Pause.*) Now —I'll go over this once more. If you have any questions, ask them. . . . From this point on you're Claire Flem-

ming. We're going to leave together and take a cab to Idlewild. Keep your talking to a minimum in the cab.

SUSAN. I'm still worried about the airport. Suppose we meet someone who knows your wife?

FLEMMING. We won't.

SUSAN. How can you be sure? I don't even look like her.

FLEMMING. People see what they expect to see. It's the principle of association. You're dressed like Claire and you're traveling with me—that means you're my wife.

SUSAN. Let's get on the plane as soon as possible.

FLEMMING. Right. We'll go straight to our seats and sit down. Then—and this is the important part—we start the argument.

SUSAN. That's going to be difficult.

FLEMMING. You're an actress, darling, improvise. You don't like my friends . . . you're sorry you decided to come along in the first place. Make sure you're heard; I want the passengers to notice us. Then say something like, "All right, if that's the way you feel, I'm not going." I'll try to reason with you, but get up, anyway. Go to the stewardess and tell her you want to leave. She'll try to calm you down, but insist. Remember, you've *got* to get off that plane before they take away the loading ramp. Is that clear? (*She nods.*) I'll stay on board. If I can, I'll strike up a conversation with the stewardess and tell her how misunderstood I am. . . . What do you do?

SUSAN. I'll go to a rest room in the terminal and change into my own clothes. Then I'll take a taxi back here. I'll leave her dress and gloves outside with the laundry and go home.

FLEMMING. Remember, don't call or try to get in touch with me. I'll call you, probably on Monday.

SUSAN. When will I see you?

FLEMMING. Not for a while. At least a week. Just get a good rest tomorrow. And don't read the papers, they'll only upset you. (*He looks at his watch.*) Ready?

SUSAN. I—think so.

FLEMMING. Then let's get started— (*Smiles.*) Mrs. Flemming.
SUSAN. (*Thoughtfully, repeating the words.*) Mrs. Flemming . . .
FLEMMING. That's your name, darling— For the rest of our lives.

(*He turns off the living room LAMPS, comes back to her, squeezes her hand; then he picks up the suitcases and throws a raincoat over his arm. She opens the door and the* TWO *of them are framed by the LIGHT from the corridor.* SUSAN *hesitates, but* FLEMMING *leads her out and closes the door softly. There is a pause; suddenly, the door opens and* FLEMMING *comes into the room; he strides to the telephone, whips out the handkerchief, and stuffs it in his breast pocket; he takes a last look around and hurries to the door.*)

CURTAIN

END OF ACT ONE

ACT TWO

SCENE 1

TIME: *Monday morning.*

PLACE: *The living room of the* FLEMMING *apartment.* CLAIRE'S *body is gone. Bright sunlight streams in through the French doors—the broken pane of glass has been replaced.*

AT RISE: *After a moment there is the sound of a key in the lock and the hall door opens.* FLEMMING *enters, carrying the suitcases. He sets them down, closes the door, and advances into the room. He goes to the French doors and looks down at the spot where* CLAIRE *had fallen. A* MAN *comes in from the bedroom, his hands in his pockets. He is lumbering and homely, of indeterminate age. The day is warm but he wears a dusty topcoat and a battered felt hat. He chews an ancient cigar and some of its ashes have descended like dandruff to his shoulders and lapels. He is constantly brushing at himself in a vain effort to be presentable. His manner is deferential, almost humble. At times he seems a bit vacant and abstracted. His name is* COLUMBO.

COLUMBO. (*Calling out.*) Doctor Flemming?
FLEMMING. (*Turns sharply.*) Who are you?
COLUMBO. Lieutenant Columbo, Doctor. Police.
FLEMMING. I don't understand. What's happened here? Where's my wife?
COLUMBO. I guess maybe you'd better sit down. I have some bad news for you.
FLEMMING. Something's happened to Claire!
COLUMBO. You sure you don't want to sit down?

FLEMMING. (*Playing it to the hilt.*) What is it? Was she in an accident?
COLUMBO. Not exactly—
FLEMMING. Tell me!
COLUMBO. (*A pause.*) Well—somebody broke in here Friday night and tried to kill her.
FLEMMING. Oh, my God! That's— (*Suddenly realizing what* COLUMBO *has just said.*) Tried to kill her?
COLUMBO. That's right, Doctor. She's lucky she's still alive.
FLEMMING. (*Dazed.*) Still alive . . . (*Recovering.*) Where is she now?
COLUMBO. In the hospital. She was taken there Saturday morning. (*Sees* FLEMMING's *concern.*) You want a drink of water or something? Some brandy?
FLEMMING. No, no, I—just want to know how she is. Is she conscious? Has she been able to say anything?
COLUMBO. Afraid not. She's been in a coma for the past two days.
FLEMMING. I've got to see her.
COLUMBO. I'd wait for a while if I were you, Doctor. I just called the hospital. They're not letting anybody in her room, not even the police.
FLEMMING. But I can't just stand around doing nothing.
COLUMBO. Not much else you can do. They said they'd give me a ring here if she shows any improvement.
FLEMMING. What—what's her condition?
COLUMBO. (*Hesitantly.*) Well—
FLEMMING. Look, I want to know the truth.
COLUMBO. Not very good, Doctor. We just hope she comes out of it long enough to talk to us.
FLEMMING. My God, I just saw her Friday night. She was—she was fine. (*He seems to make an effort to pull himself together.*) How—did it happen?
COLUMBO. Well, we figure the guy who broke in here was a thief.
FLEMMING. A thief? And he attacked Claire?

ACT II   PRESCRIPTION: MURDER   31

COLUMBO. (*Picks up paperweight, bounces it on his palm.*) Looks that way, Doctor.

FLEMMING. But this is incredible. Why wasn't I notified?

COLUMBO. Nobody knew where you were. We couldn't reach you. Your secretary said you were upstate, but you didn't leave an address.

FLEMMING. We wanted to be alone. . . .

COLUMBO. We called the authorities. It was on the radio up there.

FLEMMING. Claire—

COLUMBO. I can come back later if you want.

FLEMMING. No. You may as well tell me the rest. How did the thief get in?

COLUMBO. He climbed up on your terrace and smashed the glass on the French doors over there. (*Hefts paperweight.*) Used something heavy, probably. Maybe a flashlight. (*Sets down paperweight.*) Anyway, your wife must've heard him. The bed was rumpled so she was probably asleep. She came in here and he—he strangled her.

FLEMMING. God—

COLUMBO. Most guys, they get in a spot like that, they run. This guy was pretty cold-blooded. I mean, let's say your wife caught him taking some stuff. So he tried to kill her. But instead of getting out of here, he finished robbing the place. Now that's not usual. A guy thinks he's committed a murder, he gets on his horse. (*The cigar has developed an ash.*)

FLEMMING. (*Indicates ash tray.*) Here.

COLUMBO. Hm? Oh. Thanks. (*Taps it.*)

FLEMMING. Who found her, Lieutenant?

COLUMBO. Your maid. She let herself in Saturday morning, saw the body, and called the police. When they got here they thought your wife was dead. The medical examiner was almost ready to sign a death certificate.

FLEMMING. Was there a pulse?

COLUMBO. Yeah, but it took him five minutes to find it. He rushed her to the hospital and she's been there ever since. She's in some kinda state where she can't get oxygen. They call it, anna—anna something.

FLEMMING. Anoxic.

COLUMBO. That's right.

FLEMMING. (*Thoughtfully.*) Then she won't live. There must've been brain damage.

COLUMBO. They're doin' everything they can, Doctor.

(*The TELEPHONE rings.* FLEMMING *snaps it up.*)

FLEMMING. Hello? (*Guarded.*) Yes, this is Doctor Flemming. No, Miss Williams, I can't possibly see you today. Why don't you come in Friday at two. (*Hangs up.*) They expect me to be on call at all hours.

COLUMBO. It's the same with me, Doc.

FLEMMING. I think I will have that drink. Something for you?

COLUMBO. Thanks, but not while I'm on duty. (*Looks around.*) Anyway, we made a pretty thorough search over the week end. Can't tell for sure, but we think he got your wife's jewelry and some other things. When you get time, will you give us a list of what was stolen?

FLEMMING. Of course.

COLUMBO. We can run down the pawn shops and the fences. Something might turn up. (*He takes out a moth-eared notebook.*) Just a few questions for my report, Doctor— (*Pats himself for a pencil.*) Now, you were away for the past two days— (*Sheepishly.*) Ah—do you have a pencil? My wife gives me one every morning, but I can't seem to—

FLEMMING. (*Gives him a pen.*) Here.

COLUMBO. Thanks. . . . Now, we know you went upstate, but the police couldn't locate you.

FLEMMING. I was at a hunting lodge. The Twin Lakes, about thirty miles outside of Syracuse. It's very quiet, relaxing. They don't even have a telephone.

COLUMBO. (*Writing this down.*) Ummm.

FLEMMING. I suppose you know—what happened on the plane?

ACT II PRESCRIPTION: MURDER 33

Columbo. Uh-huh. We talked with the airline people and they said you and your wife checked in. We were really confused. Then we contacted the stewardess. She explained things.

Flemming. It's my fault. We got into an argument on the plane, something—ridiculous. I should have calmed her down. We would have gone away together and none of this would have happened.

Columbo. You couldn't have known, Doctor.

Flemming. Just a foolish argument. I never thought she'd actually leave.

Columbo. She probably came right back here and went to bed. Time of the attack must've been close to midnight. I mean, we know she was at the airport at eleven.

Flemming. Lieutenant, if I can be of any assistance—

Columbo. Well, just a couple of formalities. There's nothing we can do until we hear from the hospital. Oh, before I forget—I hope you don't mind, but I borrowed a photograph the other day.

Flemming. Photograph?

Columbo. Picture of you and your wife. I found it in the bedroom.

Flemming. I don't understand.

Columbo. We had to have something to show the stewardess. For identification.

Flemming. I see.

Columbo. She was still upstate—they don't fly back right away, you know—and we had to contact her by phone. We sent the picture up by wire-photo.

Flemming. And?

Columbo. She identified your wife. It's not a very clear picture but she recognized her.

(*The DOORBELL rings.* Flemming *and* Columbo *exchange glances, then* Flemming *goes to the door and opens it.* Dave Gordon *enters. He is a sleek, boyish-looking man, dressed conservatively in charcoal gray. His expression is concerned as he sees* Flemming.)

DAVE. Roy! I was hoping you'd be back by now. Are you all right?

FLEMMING. I guess so, Dave, under the circumstances.

DAVE. I don't know what to say. It's a terrible, terrible thing. Sybil just had lunch with Claire on Friday.

FLEMMING. I know.

DAVE. As soon as I got word I went straight to the hospital. But they wouldn't let anyone see her. . . . Roy, something puzzles me about Friday night. When I called the two of you were getting ready to leave. What happened?

FLEMMING. We had an argument on the plane and Claire decided she wasn't going. She just walked off. I shouldn't have let her—

DAVE. Don't blame yourself, you couldn't have known. (*Shakes his head.*) There's no sense to it. You live a safe, average life and then some common thief decides you've got something he wants. So he tries to take it. And somebody always gets hurt. (*Glances at* COLUMBO, *who has been shuffling around unobtrusively.*)

COLUMBO. Lieutenant Columbo.

DAVE. My name's Dave Gordon. I'm with the District Attorney's office.

COLUMBO. Yes, sir, I know.

DAVE. I'd appreciate it if you do everything you can for Doctor Flemming. He's a good friend of mine.

COLUMBO. I'll try, sir.

DAVE. (*Turns to* FLEMMING.) Roy, we'll find the man responsible for this. You have my word. As soon as Claire is better we'll get a full description. And listen—Sybil wants you to stay with us for a few days.

FLEMMING. Let me think about it, Dave.

DAVE. I understand. . . . I suppose you'll be leaving for the hospital now.

FLEMMING. Not yet. We're waiting for a call.

DAVE. Why don't you take something and lie down for a while?

FLEMMING. Well—

DAVE. You'll feel much better. We'll tell you as soon as anything happens.

FLEMMING. All right. Unless the Lieutenant has any more questions.

COLUMBO. No, Doctor. They can wait till later.

FLEMMING. Then if you'll excuse me— (*He goes into the bedroom.* DAVE *paces, then turns to* COLUMBO.)

DAVE. Any progress so far?

COLUMBO. Well, it's still kinda early, Mister Gordon. We have a few feelers out.

DAVE. Like what?

COLUMBO. Well, we've alerted all our tipsters. Won't hear from them right away—they like to wait till they have something. Then there's routine questioning—parolees, men with similar M.O.'s. All the regular channels.

DAVE. Uh-huh.

COLUMBO. Sooner or later something usually breaks.

DAVE. Let's make that sooner. Right, Lieutenant?

COLUMBO. Do my best.

DAVE. I'm sure you will. The trouble is, we can apprehend and punish, but we've no power of prevention. Sometimes I get sick of the whole book of statutes. . . . By the way, I don't have to tell you that this could be a nice feather in your cap. It's getting quite a play in the papers. Wrap it up and everybody looks good.

COLUMBO. Yes, sir.

DAVE. (*He paces.*) I wish they'd call. When was the last time you talked to the hospital? (COLUMBO *doesn't answer.*) Lieutenant?

COLUMBO. Oh, sorry. I was just thinking about something.

DAVE. What's that?

COLUMBO. Nothing important. It's just that Doctor Flemming didn't call to his wife when he came in.

DAVE. I don't follow you.

COLUMBO. I was in the bedroom checking some things and I heard him open the door. But he didn't say anything. . . . Funny how people are different. Now me, the first thing I'd do if I came home after a trip, I'd say, "Honey? You here?"

DAVE. What's your point?

COLUMBO. Point? I wasn't making any point.

DAVE. (*Slightly nettled.*) It sounded as if you were, and a rather foolish one. You just heard the man admit he had an argument with his wife. He probably still had a chip on his shoulder this morning.

COLUMBO. I was only—

DAVE. (*Interrupting.*) Lieutenant, I told you Doctor Flemming is a friend of mine, a very close friend. I hope he won't be annoyed by tactless remarks, especially at a time like this.

COLUMBO. I'm sorry, Mr. Gordon. I guess I shouldn't have mentioned it.

(*The TELEPHONE rings. They look at it and* FLEMMING *comes slowly from the bedroom. He is apprehensive.* DAVE *picks it up.*)

DAVE. Hello? No, he's indisposed. You can give me the message. (*Listens, then hangs up and looks somberly at* FLEMMING.) Claire passed away a few minutes ago. . . . She was conscious at the end. (FLEMMING *stares at him.*) If it's any consolation, Roy, the last thing she called out was your name.

(FLEMMING *sinks into a chair, feigning grief. But for a beat there is the flicker of relief on his face.*)

THE LIGHTS GO OUT

END OF SCENE 1

ACT TWO

Scene 2

TIME: *The following Friday afternoon.*

PLACE: *Doctor Flemming's reception room and office.*

AT RISE: *As the LIGHTS come up, MISS PETRIE is in Flemming's office taking dictation.*

FLEMMING. (*Dictating.*) . . . As you know, my schedule has been disrupted, so I'll be unable to read my conversion hysteria paper until early next month. If you need a fill-in, try Doctors Hess or Franklin, who have done extensive work in the field. Fondest regards, etcetera, etcetera. . . . That's all, Miss Petrie We'll clear up the other correspondence tomorrow.
MISS PETRIE. I can stay late if you'd like.
FLEMMING. That's very kind of you, Miss Petrie, but it won't be necessary.

(*The TELEPHONE rings on his desk. She answers it.*)

MISS PETRIE. Doctor Flemming's office. . . . (*Sighs.*) Oh, hello, Mr. Sussman. Just a minute, I'll see. (*Cups mouthpiece.*) He'd like to talk to you, Doctor.
FLEMMING. Tell him I just left the profession.
MISS PETRIE. (*To phone.*) Mr. Sussman? He just left —for the day. No, I'm sorry, he just went out. Would I lie to you, Mr. Sussman? . . . Really, no one's trying to avoid you. . . . You did what? With your wife? Well, I don't know if the Doctor can help you with that. (*At this point the reception room door opens and LIEUTENANT COLUMBO comes in, holding his hat in his hands. He seems bewildered by the expensive surroundings.*) Oh, yes, I'll tell him. And if your wife calls, I'll say we haven't heard from you. . . . Fine, Mr. Sussman. 'Bye-bye. (*Hangs up.*) Poor man. While you were at home he kept calling five times a day.

FLEMMING. (*Wryly.*) I don't know whether to charge him by the hour or the message unit. If we're lucky he'll run out of dimes.
MISS PETRIE. (*Taking her dictation pad.*) Well, I'll get these letters typed up.

(*She goes into the reception room, sees* COLUMBO.)

MISS PETRIE. May I help you?
COLUMBO. Is—ah, is the doctor in, Miss?
MISS PETRIE. (*Noting his rumpled attire.*) Do you have an appointment?
COLUMBO. Well, no. It's police business. Just tell him Lieutenant Columbo's here.

(*She rings* FLEMMING'S *office.*)

FLEMMING. (*Answering.*) Yes?
MISS PETRIE. There's a police officer to see you, Doctor. Lieutenant Columbo.
FLEMMING. Columbo? (*He places the name.*) Send him in.
MISS PETRIE. Go right in, Lieutenant.

(COLUMBO *nods and enters the office.* FLEMMING, *smooth and self-possessed now, rises from behind the desk and shakes hands with him.*)

FLEMMING. Hello, Lieutenant. I was hoping to hear from you. Any news?
COLUMBO. Nothing much, Doctor. We're sorta waiting around until our friend tries to get rid of the jewelry.
FLEMMING. I imagine he'd keep it for a while.
COLUMBO. Probably. (*He crosses and takes a lighter from the desk, ignites his cigar; then he looks around the office.*) First time I've ever been in a psychiatrist's office. I keep looking for the couch.
FLEMMING. (*A smile.*) You've seen too many movies, Lieutenant.

COLUMBO. (*Chuckles.*) Put me in a horizontal position, I'd fall asleep. (*He continues browsing while* FLEMMING *watches.*) Nice place, though. Restful. Guess it puts people in the mood to talk. I got a sister, she has a living room—modern, you know? . . . You sit in there and you're afraid to open your mouth. She has this big, kidney-shaped coffee table. Upsets me just to look at it. Her husband doesn't say much. I figure the coffee table got to him a couple years ago.

FLEMMING. (*Bored.*) Is there something I can do for you?

COLUMBO. Hmmm? Oh. No, not really, Doctor. I brought your pen back. (*He takes it from his pocket.*) I forgot to give it to you at the inquest.

FLEMMING. (*Takes the pen.*) Thanks.

COLUMBO. That's the trouble with me—I'm always forgetting things. I read about that in the *Reader's Digest*. Big article by some doctor. Maybe you know him, he's a psychiatrist. Anyway, he's got this theory about people with bad memories. You know anything about that?

FLEMMING. Probably the Freudian idea that there are no accidents. If you forget something it's because you want to.

COLUMBO. I hope *that's* not true. I left my wife in a bowling alley last week. (*Chuckles.*) I was halfway down the street before I remembered she was in the ladies' room.

FLEMMING. (*Trying to get him back on the subject.*) Was there anything else you wanted, Lieutenant?

COLUMBO. Well, nothing important. Just a little detail that's been bothering me.

FLEMMING. What is it?

COLUMBO. Well, about your luggage.

FLEMMING. My luggage?

COLUMBO. (*He notes his cigar has gone out; picks up the desk lighter and snaps it a few times; it doesn't light.*) I think you're out of fluid. (*A flame springs up.*) No. Guess I don't know how to work the thing. (*He leisurely lights his cigar.*)

FLEMMING. (*Annoyed.*) You were talking about my luggage.

COLUMBO. Yeah. You took two suitcases upstate, didn't you?

FLEMMING. That's right. We packed more than we needed.

COLUMBO. Uh-huh. Well, I went out to the airport the other day. You know, routine checking. It seems your suitcases were thirteen pounds overweight. They keep a record.

FLEMMING. I know. I charged it on my credit card.

COLUMBO. (*Looking for an ash tray.*) When you came back—Monday morning, right?—your luggage was only four pounds overweight. It's a stupid little point, Doctor, but—ah, I was wondering what happened to those extra nine pounds?

FLEMMING. (*A pause; he takes a cigarette from a box and carefully lights it.*) I don't quite see what this has to do with my wife's death.

COLUMBO. (*Apologetically.*) It's part of my job. I gotta make sure all the loose ends get tucked in.

FLEMMING. It seems you went to a great deal of trouble. It's a long trip out to the airport.

COLUMBO. (*Shrugs.*) Forty-five minutes. Anyway, I had something else I was working on out there. Thought I'd kill two birds with one stone. That's quite a place, that airport. Really fixed it up. I get lost just walking around.

FLEMMING. About those nine pounds, Lieutenant. I took a stack of trade journals with me and a few medical catalogues. I never have time to go through them while I'm in the office.

COLUMBO. Catchin' up on your reading?

FLEMMING. You could put it that way.

COLUMBO. You didn't bring them back, then?

FLEMMING. No, there was no reason to keep them. Advertising stuff, mostly.

COLUMBO. And you figure they weighed as much as nine pounds?

FLEMMING. They must have. Why else would there be a disparity in the weights?

COLUMBO. (*Seems satisfied.*) Yeah. Well, that clears that up. Thanks, Doctor. Sorry to bother you.

FLEMMING. No bother at all.

COLUMBO. (*He walks to the door; then he pauses and turns.*) Oh, one more thing. Do you remember what your wife was wearing last Friday night?

FLEMMING. (*Thoughtfully.*) I'm not sure. . . . Claire had so many dresses. Is it important?

COLUMBO. Well, in a way.

FLEMMING. I think it was a gray wool dress—if I'm not mistaken.

COLUMBO. Uh-huh. That's what the stewardess said. She's back in town, by the way, and I talked to her. She said your wife was wearing a gray wool dress and white gloves.

FLEMMING. Yes, I believe so.

COLUMBO. Funny, though. . . . If she came home from the airport, got undressed and put on her negligee, what did she do with her dress and gloves? We couldn't find them when we went over your apartment last week end. There was a blue wool dress and a brown wool dress, but no gray. And there were a lot of gloves—leather ones, the long kind women wear to dances—but no white ones.

FLEMMING. Perhaps they were stolen.

COLUMBO. Maybe. Did you put them on that list of stolen items?

FLEMMING. Really, Lieutenant, how could you expect me to notice they were missing?

COLUMBO. Still, it's kinda puzzling when you think of it. I mean, why would the guy take just one dress and a pair of gloves? The dress I can understand. But the gloves? What are they worth? Unless he wanted to give them to his girl, or something.

FLEMMING. I haven't the slightest idea. People don't always do the rational thing.

COLUMBO. They sure don't. You learn a lot about that in my line. Yours, too, I guess.

(SUSAN HUDSON *enters the reception room. She crosses to* MISS PETRIE.)

SUSAN. Hello.

MISS PETRIE. Hello, Miss Hudson. I'll ring the Doctor.

(*She rings Flemming's phone; he picks it up.*)

FLEMMING. Yes?

MISS PETRIE. Miss Hudson is here, Doctor.

FLEMMING. (*Pause.*) I'll be finished in a moment. (*Hangs up; to* COLUMBO.) I have a patient, Lieutenant.

COLUMBO. (*A look at his watch.*) Two o'clock. Miss Williams, right?

FLEMMING. You have quite a memory.

COLUMBO. (*Modestly brushing this aside.*) Well—it goes with the job.

FLEMMING. Sorry I couldn't help you with the dress and gloves. Perhaps you missed them in your search.

COLUMBO. You're probably right. Say, do you mind if I come over this afternoon and take another look? What time will you be home?

FLEMMING. About five.

COLUMBO. Suppose I meet you there at five-thirty?

FLEMMING. All right—if you think it's necessary.

COLUMBO. (*Smiles.*) Just another loose end, Doctor. You understand.

(FLEMMING *ushers him to the door.* SUSAN *rises as* COLUMBO *comes into the reception room.*)

MISS PETRIE. You can go in now, Miss Hudson.

SUSAN. (*She rises, starts for the door.*) Thank you.

COLUMBO. (*Suddenly turning.*) Miss?

SUSAN. (*Startled.*) Yes?

COLUMBO. (*Strolling over.*) Excuse me. What's your name again?

SUSAN. Susan Hudson. Why?

COLUMBO. Sorry to trouble you, miss.

(*He makes an awkward, deferential motion and exits.* SUSAN *hurries into Flemming's office.*)

ACT II   PRESCRIPTION: MURDER   43

SUSAN. Who was that man out there?

FLEMMING. Lieutenant Columbo. He's a police officer. Why?

SUSAN. Well, he—he wanted to know my name.

FLEMMING. (*Sharply.*) Did you tell him?

SUSAN. What else could I do? (*Sees his agitation.*) Roy, what's wrong? Do you think he suspects something?

FLEMMING. Just calm down.

SUSAN. But why should he want to know *my* name?

FLEMMING. He was in my apartment Monday when you called. I told you not to get in touch with me.

SUSAN. I had to. When I read that Claire was still alive I wanted to warn you.

FLEMMING. Columbo caught the mixup in names. But it's nothing to worry about. For all he knows Miss Petrie could have juggled my appointments. . . . Now— (*He picks up the phone.*) I'm going to call the cleaners. You did what I told you, didn't you? You left Claire's dress and gloves with the rest of the laundry?

SUSAN. Gloves—?

FLEMMING. Yes, the dress and the gloves. Susan, I told you.

(*A horrified look crosses her face.*)

FLEMMING. (*Hangs up.*) What is it?

SUSAN. I changed in one of the booths at the airport and put her things in my bag. Then I came back to your apartment and left the dress with the other laundry.

FLEMMING. Go on.

SUSAN. Well, I—I forgot all about the gloves. I didn't even think of them until you mentioned them.

FLEMMING. (*Exasperated.*) We went over it. How many times did I tell you?

SUSAN. (*Defensively.*) I'm sorry. But what difference does it make? Is it that important?

FLEMMING. *Important?* Where are the gloves now?

SUSAN. In my other bag, at home. I haven't used it since that night. (*Sees his agitation.*) Oh, Roy, I'm terribly sorry if I've messed things up.

FLEMMING. No—no—let me think. (*He paces, talking aloud.*) We're safe on the dress, it's at the cleaners. And the gloves? Well, a pair of gloves could be overlooked. They're small, they could be anywhere. (*Turns to her.*) Listen, Columbo's coming to my apartment this afternoon. He wants to make another search. Go home and get the gloves. Then take a cab to my place. I'll meet you there in half an hour.

SUSAN. Why can't I just throw them away? There's an incinerator in my building. I'll just drop them down.

FLEMMING. No. I want him to find them. He'll only be satisfied if all his damn loose ends are in place.

SUSAN. But—

FLEMMING. (*Takes her arms.*) Darling, do as I say. And hurry!

(*He opens the door for her; she looks at him for a beat, then goes out.*)

MISS PETRIE. (*Smiling at her.*) Finished already?

(SUSAN *doesn't answer; she crosses quickly to the hall door and exits.* FLEMMING *closes his office door and leans against it; then he moves decisively to the phone, picks it up, dials.*)

FLEMMING. Madison Cleaners? This is Doctor Flemming. I believe my— (*The voice at the other end of the line begins to offer saccharine condolences.*) Thank you, that's very kind of you. I was going to ask if— Yes, thanks, I appreciate it. . . . No, as far as we know she wasn't in pain. . . . Anyway, we left some laundry with you last week. If it's finished, will you send someone over with it? . . . Fine. Thank you. (*He hangs up, lights a cigarette, blows a thoughtful cloud of smoke toward the ceiling; then he turns and starts for the door.*)

THE LIGHTS GO OUT

END OF SCENE 2

ACT TWO

Scene 3

Time: *A half hour later.*

Place: *The living room of the Flemming apartment.*

At Rise: Flemming *is fixing himself a drink at the bar. The DOORBELL rings. He goes to answer it, admits* Susan.

Flemming. Did you bring them? (*She nods, opens her bag and holds out the gloves.*) Just put them on the table. I'll hide them in her bureau. (*Smiles.*) Columbo's going to find them this time. (*She drops them on the table.*) Drink?

Susan. Please. (*He begins mixing her one;* Susan *crosses to him.*) Are you angry with me?

Flemming. (*Kisses her on the side of the neck.*) Not at all.

Susan. I would have to do something foolish. I kept going over everything in my mind. But those damn gloves.

Flemming. (*Hands her the drink.*) Don't worry about it. We've protected ourselves.

(*They raise their glasses in a silent toast, drink.*)

Susan. I've missed you. I didn't think I could get through the week. Things are going to be all right, aren't they?

Flemming. Of course.

Susan. What about that man—that Columbo?

Flemming. You'll never see him again.

Susan. But why was he bothering you?

Flemming. Because in some dim way he's suspicious of me.

Susan. (*Startled.*) Suspicious?

Flemming. (*Smiles.*) Darling, I told you not to worry.

In a policeman's world you're always suspect, no matter what you do. It's like the story of the patient coming to the analytic session. If he's early he's anxious, if he's on time he's compulsive, and if he's late he's resisting. You can't win.

SUSAN. I thought we covered ourselves.

FLEMMING. We did, but Claire's death was almost too perfect. That's what irritates Columbo; it's like a speck in his eye. He'd even look for flaws in the Old Testament.

SUSAN. You don't seem very upset about it.

FLEMMING. Why should I be? No matter which way he turns I have an answer for him. So he'll keep checking until he hits one dead end after another. Eventually he'll lose interest in me and start hounding somebody else.

SUSAN. I wish I could be sure of that. (*Troubled.*) These past few days I've tried to find an excuse for what we've done. . . . I haven't been very successful.

FLEMMING. Susan, it was our only alternative. I didn't want to kill Claire, but I couldn't reach her. Our marriage was all she had, so she dug in her nails and hung on. That kind of woman can't withdraw gracefully.

SUSAN. Does that justify—?

FLEMMING. (*Interrupting, meaning it.*) Yes. We're in love with each other. That's all the justification we need. (*Takes her arms.*) Look, you're having a natural reaction. It was a terrible experience and I hated to put you through it, but I needed your help.

SUSAN. (*Quietly.*) I know.

FLEMMING. It's not something you forget, but don't let it interfere with what we have now.

SUSAN. I won't let it.

FLEMMING. We've come this far—all we have to do for the time being is wait. I promise I'll make it up to you.

SUSAN. (*Sets down her drink, hugs him.*) I just want to be with you—

(*They embrace; there is a tiny click:* SUSAN *goes stiff and* FLEMMING *jerks his head toward the door; the sound of a key scraping in the lock is audible;* FLEM-

MING *gestures toward the bedroom;* SUSAN *seems dazed. He gives her a shove and she runs into the bedroom, closing the door.* FLEMMING *strides to the hall door and waits. After a beat it opens;* LIEUTENANT COLUMBO *is bent down, a key in the lock. He comes into the room, then suddenly glances up and sees* FLEMMING.)

COLUMBO. (*Startled and flustered.*) Oh!—Ah—Doctor Flemming.

FLEMMING. (*Coldly.*) What are you doing here?

COLUMBO. (*Acutely embarrassed.*) Well—ah—I thought I'd kinda save you some time and look for the stuff myself. You know. No sense inconveniencing you any more than I have to. The superintendent gave me the key.

FLEMMING. Don't you people usually require a search warrant?

COLUMBO. (*Innocently.*) I didn't think it would be necessary, Doctor. I mean, you gave me your permission, didn't you? (*Pause.*) Say, how come you're back here now?

FLEMMING. Because it bothered me, too. I wanted to save us both some time. (*Points to table.*) There are the gloves, Lieutenant. I found them in one of her bureau drawers.

(COLUMBO *crosses to the table and picks them up.* FLEMMING *suddenly notices* SUSAN'S *glass sitting on the bar. Before* COLUMBO *can see it, he moves between the glass and the police officer's line of vision.*)

COLUMBO. How do you like that? We covered every inch of that bureau. Guess we missed these. You didn't find the dress by any chance, did you?

FLEMMING. No. I turned the place upside down. It's not here.

COLUMBO. Wonder what she did with it?

FLEMMING. I'm afraid I have no idea.

COLUMBO. (*Glancing toward bedroom.*) Why don't we both give another look? (*He starts for bedroom door.*)

FLEMMING. Lieutenant, it's not in this apartment. I went through all the closets.
COLUMBO. There's a laundry hamper in the bathroom, isn't there?
FLEMMING. But I just told you—
COLUMBO. No harm in checking it out.

(*He reaches the bedroom door, puts his hand on the knob; the front DOORBELL rings;* COLUMBO *turns.*)

FLEMMING. (*Smoothly.*) Will you get that, Lieutenant? I don't want to talk to anyone.

(COLUMBO *hesitates, but the BELL rings again. He crosses to the hall door. The moment his back is to* FLEMMING, *the* DOCTOR *pours out* SUSAN'S *drink, sets the glass behind the bar.*)

COLUMBO. (*Opening the door.*) Yes?

(*A young* DELIVERY BOY *stands outside with a box and a paper-covered hanger.*)

BOY. Madison Cleaners.
FLEMMING. (*Greatly relieved, he strides to the door.*) How much do I owe you?
BOY. Two-sixty.
FLEMMING. (*Paying him.*) Keep the change.

(*The* BOY *goes out and* FLEMMING *moves to the center of the room, tears the paper from the hanger;* CLAIRE'S *dress is inside. He drapes it across a chair, then turns and looks at* COLUMBO.)

COLUMBO. Say, that's your wife's dress, isn't it?
FLEMMING. That's right. When she came back from the airport she must have left it outside for the cleaners.
COLUMBO. Yeah, it matches the description. Mind if I take a look?

ACT II   PRESCRIPTION: MURDER   49

(FLEMMING *picks up a magnifying glass, drops it in front of* COLUMBO.)

FLEMMING. (*Sarcastically.*) Take a good look. (*They exchange glances; then:*) Now if you don't mind, I have to get back to my office. We've both been wasting our time.

COLUMBO. Sorry about all this. I seem to be making a pest of myself. (FLEMMING *doesn't answer.* COLUMBO *shuffles to the door, then turns.*) Hey, you might get a kick outta this, Doc. A few hours ago somebody confessed.

FLEMMING. What?

COLUMBO. Yeah. Young kid walked into the office and said he killed your wife.

FLEMMING. Why didn't you tell me this before?

COLUMBO. Well, I didn't think it was important. He was just some kid off the streets. We questioned him and he fell apart. (*Shakes his head.*) They come in after every murder. You know, the kooks and the old ladies. I guess they want to get their names in the papers.

FLEMMING. Are you sure this boy didn't do it?

COLUMBO. Positive. He didn't even know what was stolen. (*Thoughtfully.*) Not a bad kid, though. Maybe he had a girl friend he wanted to impress. Seemed real disappointed when we told him to go home. (FLEMMING *has been standing impatiently near the open door;* COLUMBO *notes this.*) Well, I'll be going. (*He moves toward the door, pauses again.*) Oh, that reminds me. That hunting lodge upstate. There's a lake nearby, isn't there?

FLEMMING. (*An edge of sarcasm.*) Considering the fact I told you the lodge is called Twin Lakes, I'd say that was an informed guess.

COLUMBO. Do any fishing while you were up there?

FLEMMING. A little. Why?

COLUMBO. Nothing. I'm just a bug on fishing. My wife and I are looking for a good place to take a vacation this summer. (*Reflectively.*) Trouble with the lakes around here, people are always dumping all kinds of stuff off the boats. It's a shame. You know, cans, cigarettes, bottles. I always wondered what would happen if you could drain the water out and take a look at the bottom. Bet you'd be surprised at what you'd find. (*Pause.*) Tell me, those lakes up there, the ones where you fished. Are they mud-bottom or stone-bottom?

FLEMMING. Lieutenant, for the past week you've been asking what at best could be called irrelevant questions. I'm getting a little tired of them.

COLUMBO. I'm sorry, Doctor. I only meant you can't find bass in a mud-bottom lake. If you were fishing for bass.

FLEMMING. (*Controlled, but angry.*) What the hell does bass have to do with this? You seem to be concentrating on everything but the man who broke in here. Is this some new type of police procedure?

COLUMBO. Doctor, I just—

FLEMMING. (*Interrupting.*) I want my wife's murderer. And all this business with fish and lakes and dresses and gloves is totally non-essential.

COLUMBO. I'm only—

FLEMMING. (*Interrupting again.*) I know. You're doing your job. You're tying up loose ends. Well, spend a little less time with loose ends and you might come up with something important. Now I've been patient with you, but there's a limit. (*Pause.*) Sometimes I almost get the impression you think *I* killed Claire.

COLUMBO. You? No. How could you? You were on your way upstate.

FLEMMING. I'm glad you remembered that. (*Pause.*) Unless you think I hired someone to kill her. That boy who confessed. Maybe I paid *him* to do it.

COLUMBO. No, you didn't do that, Doctor.

FLEMMING. How do you know?

COLUMBO. (*Evenly.*) I already asked him.

(*He studies* FLEMMING *for a moment, then leaves.* FLEMMING *slams the door. He stands motionless. Then, with quiet anger, he strides to the telephone and dials a number.*)

FLEMMING. (*To phone.*) Hello, I'd like to speak to Dave Gordon, please. . . . Yes. Tell him Doctor Flemming's calling. . . . (*He waits, drums his fingers impatiently.* SUSAN *comes slowly from the bedroom.*) Hello, Dave? Roy. . . . Not bad, thanks. Listen, Dave, I've got a little problem here. Do you remember that police lieutenant you met last week, the one assigned to the case? . . . That's right, Columbo. Well, Dave, the man's been making an absolute pest of himself. He keeps calling, dropping by, annoying me at the office. It's getting ridiculous. . . . Frankly, Dave, I was wondering if there was something you could do. . . . Well, you know, pull a few strings. . . . Exactly. . . . Fine, Dave. Well, I *would* appreciate it. . . .

SLOW CURTAIN

END OF ACT TWO

ACT THREE

SCENE 1

TIME: *Late that afternoon.*

PLACE: *The reception room and office of Doctor Flemming.*

AT RISE: *It is growing dark, and LIGHTS burn in the reception room and Flemming's office.* MISS PETRIE *is adjusting her hat with the aid of a small hand mirror. She closes her purse and goes to the connecting door, looks in.* FLEMMING *is putting papers in his attaché case.*

MISS PETRIE. I'm leaving now, Doctor. Good night.
FLEMMING. Good night. (*She turns to go.*) Oh, Miss Petrie— (*As she turns back.*) I forgot to tell you. Miss Hudson is coming in tomorrow morning at ten.
MISS PETRIE. I'll put it in the book.
FLEMMING. Thank you. Good night.

(MISS PETRIE *goes to her desk and makes a notation in her appointment book; she closes it and leaves.* FLEMMING *walks to his bookcase, scans the titles for one he wants, and drops it in the attaché case. He secures the case and snaps off his desk lamp. While he is doing this, the door to the outer office opens and* COLUMBO *enters. He strolls to Miss Petrie's desk and stands there, lighting his cigar.* FLEMMING, *on his way out, comes from his office; he is preoccupied.*)

COLUMBO. Evening, Doctor.
FLEMMING. (*Rousing at the sound of the voice.*) What do you want?

ACT III   PRESCRIPTION: MURDER   53

COLUMBO. Nothing important. I just dropped by to tell you some news. Thought you might be interested.

FLEMMING. What's that?

COLUMBO. I got taken off the case today. I'm not workin' on it any more.

FLEMMING. (*A pause.*) Oh?

COLUMBO. Yeah. Happened all of a sudden, too. I was sitting at my desk and a call came down from upstairs. They said they decided to put me on something else. Real strange, y'know? And they said I was to turn my files over to Lieutenant Green. He's a nice fella, but he's a little young. Hasn't had much experience in this kinda thing. Funny . . . (*Puzzled.*) Here I thought I was doing a good job—

FLEMMING. (*Now that he knows his phone call has worked, he's no longer interested.*) That's unfortunate, Lieutenant, but I suppose they know what they're doing. You'll have to excuse me now. I have a dinner engagement.

COLUMBO. At the Gordons?

FLEMMING. Why do you say that?

COLUMBO. Well, Mister Gordon's a friend of yours, isn't he? I mean, when we were at your apartment last week he invited you over. Remember?

FLEMMING. It isn't with Mister Gordon.

COLUMBO. (*Has opened the appointment book and is casually leafing through it.*) A lady friend, maybe?

FLEMMING. I don't think that's any of your business.

COLUMBO. No, I guess not. (*Closes book.*) I was wondering, Doctor . . . Maybe you'd like to take me on as a patient.

FLEMMING. What?

COLUMBO. You might be able to give me some help. I don't know, there must be something wrong with me. I seem to bother people, I make them nervous. Maybe you can tell me why.

FLEMMING. You can't be serious.

(COLUMBO *strolls into the other office, apparently deeply*

involved in what he is saying. FLEMMING *follows, snapping on the LIGHT.*)

COLUMBO. My wife says I ought to have it looked into. So I told her I know a psychiatrist. And I figure if I come to you, say once a week, we could get it ironed out. You know what I think the problem is? (FLEMMING *doesn't answer.*) I think I'm too suspicious. I just don't trust people, that's my trouble. (*A thought occurs to him.*) For instance, I get taken off a case, I figure somebody put pressure on. Isn't that stupid? And if somebody puts pressure on, I gotta ask myself why. What do you think, Doctor?

FLEMMING. (*Quietly.*) I think you should get out of here.

COLUMBO. (*Surprised.*) Beg pardon?

FLEMMING. Columbo, you're a public servant. You say you're off the case? Fine. If you bother me again, I'll have to call your superior.

COLUMBO. You're making a lot of phone calls today, aren't you, Doctor?

(FLEMMING *looks at him angrily for a long moment; then, abruptly, his mood changes—something about the little man, some wry aspect of his personality, appeals to the doctor's sense of the ludicrous; he starts to chuckle; finally he is laughing out loud.* COLUMBO *is baffled; then he too begins to grin.*)

FLEMMING. (*Good-naturedly.*) Columbo, you're magnificent. You really are.

COLUMBO. (*Chuckling.*) Why do you say that, Doc?

FLEMMING. (*Claps him on the back.*) You are by far the most persistent bastard I've ever met. But you're likable. The astonishing thing is that you're likable. Did anyone ever tell you you were droll?

COLUMBO. Me?

FLEMMING. Well, you are. Droll as hell.

COLUMBO. Come on now, Doc—

FLEMMING. (*Still highly amused.*) You're a sly elf, Columbo. You should sit under your own private toadstool. You were thrown off the case and yet you have the flaming audacity to come back here and bother me. I respect that. It's irritating, but I respect it. How about a drink?

COLUMBO. (*He wants one.*) Well—

(FLEMMING *pulls back a section of the books and reveals a concealed bar. He begins mixing drinks.*)

COLUMBO. Hey, that's pretty clever. You can take a snort between patients.

FLEMMING. I haven't given you a Rorschach yet, but I have a hunch you're a bourbon man. (*Hands him drink.*)

COLUMBO. Thanks, Doc.

FLEMMING. What shall we drink to?

COLUMBO. (*Thinks.*) Well—how about you and me?

FLEMMING. Fine.

(*They touch glasses,* FLEMMING *sardonically,* COLUMBO *apparently unaware of the mockery in the toast. The* POLICE OFFICER'S *attention wanders to the books; he takes one out, then slips it back, turns to* FLEMMING.)

COLUMBO. Say—you ever read any murder mysteries?

FLEMMING. (*Indulgently.*) No, afraid not.

COLUMBO. Me, I love 'em. Nice and relaxing, you know? Trouble is, they're nothing like real life. I mean, the guy who did it, they catch him every time. Now we both know it doesn't always work that way.

FLEMMING. (*Amused.*) You never stop, do you?

COLUMBO. What?

FLEMMING. The insinuations, the change of pace. You're a bag of tricks, Columbo. (*Laughs.*) Right down to that prop cigar you use.

COLUMBO. (*Sheepishly.*) Well—

FLEMMING. I'm going to tell you something about yourself. You said you needed a psychiatrist. Maybe you do and maybe you don't. But you're a perfect example of compensation. (*Pours more liquor in* COLUMBO's *glass.*)

COLUMBO. Of what, Doc?

FLEMMING. Compensation. Adaptability. You're an intelligent man, Columbo. But you hide it, you play the clown. Why? Because of your appearance. You think you'll never get by on looks or polish, so you make a defect into a virtue. You take people by surprise. They underestimate you and that's how you trip them up. Like coming here tonight.

COLUMBO. Boy, you really got me pegged. Gotta watch myself with you, Doc. You're pretty good at figuring people out.

FLEMMING. (*A smile.*) Now you're trying flattery.

COLUMBO. (*Protesting.*) No, I'm serious. Really. You've got a gift, Doc. Sure, I know it's your job and you've studied it for years, but it's still kinda amazing. A person sits in this chair for a couple hours and you know all about him.

FLEMMING. Not quite. Psychiatry isn't a parlor trick.

COLUMBO. Oh, I didn't mean that. I got a lotta respect for psychiatrists. I was just wondering— (*Thinks for a beat; then.*) No, I guess it isn't possible.

FLEMMING. What?

COLUMBO. Well, it's easy enough to figure out a patient. Or somebody like me who's hanging around all the time. But what about a stranger, a guy you've never met? Can you tell what makes him tick?

FLEMMING. (*Ahead of him.*) Anyone particular in mind?

COLUMBO. No, nobody special. Just a type.

FLEMMING. (*Smiling.*) Like a murderer, for instance?

COLUMBO. Well, yeah, now that you mention it. I guess we're on the same wave length.

FLEMMING. I guess we are. (*He refills their glasses.*) What about this hypothetical murderer?

COLUMBO. Well, I'm not talking about the average hothead. You know, the guy who pops somebody on the noggin with a bottle. I mean the kind of man who thinks the whole thing through, step by step. He sorta makes up a blueprint and follows it. What's he like, Doc?

FLEMMING. (*Amused.*) I should charge you for this. But since it's on a theoretical basis, let's just call it a free consultation. (*He picks up his glass, toys with it reflectively.*) All right, we're talking about a man who commits a crime—not the garden variety of barroom brawl—but an elaborate intellectual project. What do we know about this man? Well, you said he's working from a blueprint, so he's obviously not impulsive. He plans, he calculates, he minimizes risks. That shows the discipline of a damn fine brain. He's oriented by his mind, not his viscera. Probably well educated, too.

COLUMBO. Like, maybe, a professional man?

FLEMMING. (*Smiles.*) Perhaps. (*He is talking about himself and they both know it; but even though he is fencing with* COLUMBO, *the sheer force of his ego shows through.*) At any rate— (*He straightens something on his desk.*) an orderly man, a man with an eye for detail. And courage.

COLUMBO. Courage?

FLEMMING. Certainly. You can't go through something like this—whatever it may be, without a strong nervous system.

COLUMBO. Yeah, I guess. But one thing bothers me, Doc. This guy we're talking about, he's taken a human life. (*A pause.*) Wouldn't you say he's insane?

FLEMMING. Why? Because he's committed an immoral act? Morals are conditioned, Lieutenant. They're relative, like everything else these days. Our murderer can be as sane as you— (*Slight smile.*) or me. He's just a believer in the art of the possible. Let's say he has a limited range of choices in a given situation. If one of them is murder —well, murder may be repugnant to him, but if it's the only solution, he uses it. That's pragmatism, not insanity.

COLUMBO. Tell me something, Doc. How do you catch a man like that?

FLEMMING. You don't.

COLUMBO. (*Nodding glumly.*) Yeah, you're probably right. He sounds too clever for us. I mean, cops aren't the brightest guys in the world. 'Course, we got something going for us—we're professionals. (*Thoughtfully.*) Now you take our friend, this murderer. Sure, he's smart all right, but he's an amateur. He's got one chance to learn, just one. With us—well, it's a business. We go through this thing a hundred times a year. That's a lot of practice, Doc.

FLEMMING. (*Amiably.*) In your case it hasn't helped, has it? All that experience and you've jumped to the wrong conclusion.

COLUMBO. What d'you mean?

FLEMMING. I didn't kill my wife.

COLUMBO. (*Surprised.*) I never said you did.

FLEMMING. No, that's true. Infer is more the word. But if I *did* kill her—and I said if—you'd have one hell of a time proving it. So why don't we part friends? You go on to something new and I'll forget this whole thing. There's really no reason for us to see each other again. (*Looks at his watch.*) And now I have to get going.

COLUMBO. I'll go down with you.

FLEMMING. No. Finish your drink. Relax. Search the office. And if the cleaning woman comes in—just show her your badge. (*He starts for the door, pauses.*) And, Lieutenant—if you want to smoke—open the window. Good night.

(FLEMMING *goes out.* COLUMBO *waits until the outer door closes and sets down his drink. His face blank, he goes into the reception room and begins paging methodically through the appointment book. He finds what he wants, then picks up the phone and dials.*)

COLUMBO. (*To phone.*) Hello? Who's this, Fred? Columbo. Listen, I want a pick-up. Girl named Susan Hudson, the Flemming case. No, I don't know the address. It's in my file, though. Get a car down there now. I want her in my office tonight. And, Fred—don't let her make any phone calls. (*He hangs up reflectively and starts for the door.*)

THE LIGHTS GO OUT

END OF SCENE 1

ACT THREE

Scene 2

TIME: *Later that night.*

PLACE: *The office of* LIEUTENANT COLUMBO *at police headquarters.*

AT RISE: SUSAN HUDSON *is alone in the room, nervously stubbing out a cigarette in an ash tray. She looks over at the door, where a policeman's shadow looms against the glass. Then she sits down and lights another cigarette. Finally, she crosses to* COLUMBO'S *desk, picks up the phone, begins dialing. Apparently the operator cuts in on the line.*

SUSAN. Hello? . . . No, I don't want the switchboard, I want an outside line. (*Annoyed.*) Well, you keep cutting in every time I dial. Just put me through to an outside operator, will you? . . . Official permission? To make a phone call? Oh, for God's sake. . . . No, I don't want to talk to the desk sergeant!

(*She slams down the phone, crushes out the cigarette. The door opens and* LIEUTENANT COLUMBO *comes in. She turns.*)

COLUMBO. Hello, Miss Hudson.
SUSAN. Who are you?

COLUMBO. Lieutenant Columbo. I met you the other day, remember?

SUSAN. Are you responsible for bringing me down here?

COLUMBO. Yes, ma'am.

SUSAN. Well, this is the most— I've never heard of anything like this before. Do you know I've been waiting here for half an hour? I couldn't even make a phone call. Every time I dialed the operator got on the line.

COLUMBO. (*Sheepishly.*) They kinda clamp down on calls after six o'clock, ma'am. Some type of economy drive, I guess. And I'm sorry I kept you waiting. I was out gettin' coffee.

SUSAN. Well, would you mind telling me why I'm here?

COLUMBO. Sure. Just wanted to ask you a few routine questions. I thought you might be able to help us with a case we've been working on. (*He moves to his desk and begins rearranging papers.*)

SUSAN. What case is that? (*He seems lost in his papers.*) Lieutenant?

COLUMBO. (*Without looking up.*) The Flemming case.

SUSAN. (*Carefully.*) You mean Doctor Flemming? My psychiatrist?

COLUMBO. Uh-huh.

SUSAN. Is he in some sort of trouble?

COLUMBO. (*Still intent on the papers.*) What?

SUSAN. I said, is he in some sort of trouble?

COLUMBO. Well, in a way. (*He looks at her finally.*) Sit down, Miss Hudson. (*Slowly, she sits.* COLUMBO *begins to pace, letting silence expand for a moment. He takes out a cigar stub and lights it.*) It won't bother you if I smoke, will it?

SUSAN. No.

COLUMBO. Some women don't like the smell of cigars. My wife prefers a pipe. I could never get used to one, though. Too much stuff to carry around. (*Pause.*) How long have you known the doctor?

SUSAN. You mean how long has he been treating me?

COLUMBO. Same thing, isn't it?

SUSAN. I've been seeing him for about a year.

ACT III PRESCRIPTION: MURDER 61

Columbo. Uh-huh. A year. When was the last time you talked to him, by the way?

Susan. Last week. When I met you.

Columbo. Oh, that's right.

Susan. Lieutenant, would you mind explaining—

Columbo. (*Interrupting.*) You're an actress, aren't you?

Susan. (*Startled.*) How did you know that?

Columbo. Oh, just a guess. You working here in town?

Susan. I'm rehearsing in a new play.

Columbo. Really? I'll have to see it. What kind of part have you got? I mean, a young girl, an older woman?

Susan. What does this have to do with Doctor Flemming?

Columbo. Beg pardon?

Susan. Lieutenant, you're not being very clear. You brought me all the way down here to ask me about a man I hardly know. You said he was in trouble. Now before we go on, suppose you tell me what kind of trouble.

Columbo. Well—I know this is gonna come as a shock to you, Miss Hudson. But we think— (*He pauses, studies her; then, quietly:*) we think he killed his wife.

Susan. (*Stunned.*) What?

Columbo. You seem surprised.

Susan. Of course I'm surprised. I don't believe it.

Columbo. No? Well, I guess it is kinda hard. (*He goes over toward his desk, apparently sees something lying among the papers. He reaches out and picks up a pair of sun glasses.*) Wonder who left these here? (*Holds them up; to* Susan:) They yours?

Susan. (*Sharply.*) No.

Columbo. (*Begins tapping them on his palm as he crosses to her.*) Hell of a thing to find on your desk. Maybe one of the sergeants left them. (*Stops tapping, studies her.*) What's wrong, Miss Hudson? You look a little nervous. Haven't you seen a pair of sun glasses before? (*Holds them out.*) Why don't you put them on?

Susan. (*Recoiling.*) Why should I?

COLUMBO. No reason. No reason why you shouldn't, either. (*Pause.*) Is there?
SUSAN. (*Rising.*) I think I'd better go.
COLUMBO. Sit down, Miss Hudson.
SUSAN. If you insist on keeping me here, I'm going to call my lawyer.
COLUMBO. (*Strong.*) Sit down!
SUSAN. (*Defiantly.*) You can't stop me from calling my lawyer! You have no right to order me around. You're not even on this case any more!
COLUMBO. (*Calmly.*) How did you know that?
SUSAN. (*Hesitates.*) Doctor Flemming told me.
COLUMBO. But you said you haven't seen him since last week.
SUSAN. He—called me.
COLUMBO. Oh? Is the doctor in the habit of doing that?
SUSAN. I'm not going to answer any more of your questions.
COLUMBO. Just to clear things up on one point, Miss Hudson: I *am* on the case. Somebody was pulling a few strings, all right. But my superior doesn't like that. Gets him thinking. So he says to me, "Columbo, you must be touching a sore spot somewhere. Keep at it." Very intelligent man, my superior.
SUSAN. I want to call my lawyer.
COLUMBO. Now, that doesn't figure. Doctor Flemming killed his wife and *you* want to call your lawyer. Explain that to me, Miss Hudson.
SUSAN. (*Strained.*) I want to call my lawyer.
COLUMBO. (*Pause.*) All right. (*Indicates phone.*) Go ahead. (*She looks at him for a long moment, then she rises and crosses to the desk. She picks up the telephone.*) If he wants to know the charge, it's accessory to murder. (*She hesitates.*) Make your call, Miss Hudson. Then we'll take a drive.
SUSAN. A drive?
COLUMBO. We'll go and see the stewardess. Of course, I don't have the gray wool dress, or the gloves, and you

won't put on the sun glasses, but maybe she'l remember you.

Susan. (*Hangs up, anguished.*) I don't know what you're talking about! You're trying to confuse me! I have nothing to do with this!

Columbo. With what?

Susan. With the—with this—with the thing you said about—about Roy.

Columbo. Roy?

Susan. Doctor Flemming!

Columbo. But you just called him "Roy."

Susan. What difference does that make? I *know* him. He's my doctor!

Columbo. Your lover?

Susan. Damn you, my *doctor!*

Columbo. And you never met his wife?

Susan. No, I never met his wife!

Columbo. Would you like to see some pictures of her? I had them taken at the morgue. They're in that drawer.

Susan. No!

Columbo. I guess you wouldn't. After all, you saw the real thing. That must have been quite a shock.

Susan. Why don't leave me alone? I didn't do anything.

Columbo. (*Pressing.*) No? What about the sun glasses? And those lakes upstate? And that argument on the plane?

Susan. (*Covering her ears.*) I won't listen to this!

Columbo. You were there when he strangled her, weren't you?

Susan. No!

Columbo. You mean you came later?

Susan. No! I was never there at all.

Columbo. (*Building.*) I think you were. I think you probably changed into her dress while she was lying there. Then you went to the airport with him and had that fake argument on the plane. Didn't you?

Susan. No!

Columbo. *Didn't you?* Plan it with him, help him

carry it out? You could have said no. Without you he couldn't have done it. Without you his wife would be alive right now!

SUSAN. (*Screaming.*) Stop it!!

COLUMBO. (*Pauses, sensing she has broken; his voice becomes soft and comforting.*) Why don't I have a stenographer come in? You can make a statement.

SUSAN. (*A supreme effort of will.*) No! Damn you, you have no right! (*Strained, a monotone.*) I have nothing to do with this. Do you understand? Nothing. Nothing at all. . . . If you want to take me to the stewardess, then take me. If you want to arrest me, go ahead. But you can't prove anything. Now I want to go home. You tell your men to take me home.

(*There is a long silence.* COLUMBO *sighs deeply, surprised and disappointed. Finally, he picks up his desk phone*)

COLUMBO. Fred? Send a car around for Miss Hudson, will you? (*He hangs up. To* SUSAN.) You can go. (*Quickly, without looking back, she gets up and goes to the door.*) Miss Hudson— (*She stops and he crosses to her. His voice is controlled, quiet, but it hints of anger and frustration.*) I hope you know this is only the beginning. . . . In a way, I feel sorry for you. From now on I'm gonna do everything I can to break you down. Understand? Flemming made one mistake, and that's you. You're the weak link, Miss Hudson. Tonight you surprised me, you were strong. But there's always tomorrow. And the day after that. And the day after that. Sooner or later you're gonna come back here and talk to me. And until you do, you're gonna be followed, you're gonna be hounded, you're gonna be questioned. You can't call Doctor Flemming because I have his phone tapped; you can't meet with him because I'll know about it. So you're on your own, Miss Hudson. I'll get him through you— that's a promise. (*He stops talking; she has not turned to look at him once. Finally, realizing he has finished, she*

ACT III PRESCRIPTION: MURDER 65

fumbles for the knob, opens the door, and goes quickly out. COLUMBO *lumbers back to his swivel chair, sits down; he tips back and looks morosely at the ceiling.*)

THE LIGHTS GO OUT

END OF SCENE 2

ACT THREE

SCENE 3

TIME: *The following morning.*

PLACE: *The reception room and office of Doctor Flemming.*

AT RISE: MISS PETRIE *is at her desk typing.* FLEMMING *is in his office opening his attaché case. He takes out a gold-wrapped jewelry box and sets it on top of the case. Then he writes something on a white card and slips it under the red ribbon securing the box. Finally, he glances at his watch, gets up, and crosses to the connecting door. He opens it and looks out.*

FLEMMING. Miss Petrie?
MISS PETRIE. Yes, Doctor?
FLEMMING. Doesn't Miss Hudson have a ten o'clock appointment?
MISS PETRIE. (*Checks her book.*) Yes, she does.
FLEMMING. It's almost ten-thirty. Why don't you give her a call?

(*She picks up the phone and dials. He goes back into his office, sits behind his desk.*)

MISS PETRIE. (*To phone.*) Hello? Is Miss Hudson there? . . . What? (*Startled.*) Well, no, I . . . This is the recepionist at Doctor Flemming's office. . . . Well, she had an appointment here this morning. . . . I see. (*She hangs up, disturbed, and knocks on Flemming's door.*)

FLEMMING. Come in.

MISS PETRIE. (*Looking in.*) Doctor, I called Miss Hudson, but a man answered the phone. He said he was from the coroner's office.

FLEMMING. What?

MISS PETRIE. He said there had been an accident, wanted to know who I was.

FLEMMING. What kind of an accident?

MISS PETRIE. He didn't say. He was very abrupt.

FLEMMING. Call back. Maybe you got a wrong number.

MISS PETRIE. Yes, Doctor.

(*Leaving his door partially open, she goes back to her desk. LIEUTENANT COLUMBO comes into the office; he is unshaven and disheveled-looking. He blinks at her, as if trying to marshal his thoughts; then he moves heavily toward FLEMMING'S door.*)

MISS PETRIE. Can I help you? (COLUMBO *ignores her, starts into the office.*) Wait! You can't go—

(*But he has already closed the door; he stands there stolidly until FLEMMING looks up and sees him.*)

FLEMMING. (*Irritated.*) What the hell are you doing here again?

COLUMBO. (*Wearily.*) Business, Doctor.

FLEMMING. Business? I thought we cleared that up yesterday (*Studies him.*) What's wrong with you? You look terrible.

COLUMBO. I didn't go to bed last night.

FLEMMING. Well, if you've got something on your mind, tell me. I have a full schedule this morning.

COLUMBO. (*Flat.*) Do you, Doctor?

FLEMMING. (*Puzzled.*) What is this? Look, I'm expecting a patient.

COLUMBO. Who?
FLEMMING. Is this another one of your—?
COLUMBO. (*Interrupting.*) If it's Susan Hudson, she's not coming.
FLEMMING. (*Pauses, senses the serious tone of* COLUMBO'S *voice.*) What do you mean? (COLUMBO *is silent, looking at the floor.*) I said, what do you mean? Why isn't she coming?
COLUMBO. (*A pause; then, thickly.*) She took her life last night.
FLEMMING. (*Shocked.*) What!
COLUMBO. She swallowed a bottle of sleeping pills. A whole bottle. I didn't think— (*He trails off.*)
FLEMMING. (*Sharply.*) You didn't think what? What do you have to do with this!
COLUMBO. (*Won't meet his eyes.*) I had her brought in for questioning. She—
FLEMMING. (*Hotly.*) Questioning! You damn fool. You had no right!
COLUMBO. (*Flaring.*) I know! (*Subsides, almost to himself.*) Don't you think I know?
FLEMMING. (*Tightly.*) What happened?
COLUMBO. I must have pushed her too far—I told her —I said I was gonna get to you through her.
FLEMMING. (*Through his teeth.*) You idiot!
COLUMBO. She went back to her apartment and stuffed herself with barbiturates. We got a call. . . . Took her to the hospital, pumped her stomach. . . . It was too late. (*A long pause; then, with heavy irony.*) She didn't break, Doctor. I kept after her, but she didn't break. You would have been proud of her.

(FLEMMING *stares at him; then he strides to the connecting door and snaps it open.*)

FLEMMING. Miss Petrie! Did you make that call?
MISS PETRIE. I tried, Doctor, but the line was busy.
FLEMMING. Try it again!

(*She checks her book and dials nervously with a pencil.*)

MISS PETRIE. (*To phone.*) Hello, this is Doctor Flemming's office again. Is Miss Hudson there? . . . No, you don't seem to understand. She had an appointment here this morning. . . . No, Doctor Flemming is her psychiatrist. Well, I'm just trying to get some information.

FLEMMING. (*Takes the phone from her.*) This is Doctor Flemming. Who are you, please? . . . Look, Miss Hudson was under my care. Would you mind telling me what happened? . . . Damn it, I'm her psychiatrist! . . . What kind of accident? (*Angry.*) Well, who can I call to find out? Can't you get it through your head that I want information? . . . Never mind! (*He slams down the phone and goes into his office.* COLUMBO *is sitting on one of the chairs, his face gray with fatigue.* FLEMMING *grabs the desk phone and dials a number. To phone.*) Is Dave Gordon in? Doctor Flemming calling. . . . Yes, I'll wait. (*He twists the phone cord around his fingers.*) Come on, come on! (*Then:*) Dave? Roy. Dave, listen, you have to do me a favor. It's an emergency. Call over to the police desk or the coroner's office—I don't know which. Get them to read you last night's accident sheet. . . . No, I'm checking on a patient, a Miss Susan Hudson. Susan Hudson. . . . I'm not sure, Dave. Just check it, will you? . . . Yes, I'll hold on. (*He waits.* COLUMBO *hasn't moved. Finally,* FLEMMING *begins to pace around the desk in frustration.* COLUMBO *looks up and their eyes meet; both are silent. Then:*) Yes, Dave! (*He listens.*) There's no mistake? (*After a pause, hoarsely.*) Oh, my God. . . . (*His face twists and he slowly cradles the phone. He slumps behind his desk and shields his eyes with his hands.* COLUMBO *goes over to him, stands looking down.*)

COLUMBO. Congratulations, Doctor. (FLEMMING's *head snaps up, his eyes burning.*) I mean, you're safe now, aren't you? She was the only one who could have given you away. Worked out real nice. I can't touch you any more; nobody can. You're free and clear, Doctor—you've won.

ACT III   PRESCRIPTION: MURDER

FLEMMING. (*Getting to his feet violently.*) You're responsible for this! You killed her!

COLUMBO. (*Cold.*) If I did, I have you to thank for it, don't I?

FLEMMING. (*Bitterly.*) Why didn't you leave her alone? Working on me wasn't enough! You had to bring her into it. Couldn't you tell what she'd do? Or didn't you care!

COLUMBO. (*Angry.*) You bastard, don't you lecture me! (*He thrusts his face close to* FLEMMING'S.) Yeah, I'm responsible, Doc! And I have to live with it. But you're leavin' somebody out. We *both* killed that girl, the two of us together! She committed suicide for one reason—to protect you! For you, Doc. All for you.

FLEMMING. I loved her!

COLUMBO. (*He has regained his temper.*) Yeah. Sure. (*He sighs deeply, turns away.*) Well, you won't be seeing me any more. . . . Like I said, congratulations. (*He goes toward the door.*)

FLEMMING. Wait a minute. (COLUMBO *stops.* FLEMMING *crosses to him with the air of having made a decision.*) I'm going with you.

COLUMBO. (*Surprised.*) Why?

FLEMMING. (*Quietly.*) I want to make a statement.

COLUMBO. (*Staring at him.*) That's a pretty foolish thing to do, isn't it?

FLEMMING. Maybe. . . . I doubt if you'd understand. Susan would, but not you. You see, I think I owe her something. (*Pauses for a moment.*) It's funny. . . . You have the mind of a bureaucrat, Columbo—you went after me in the wrong way. You got all tangled up in your loose ends, but you never saw the reason behind things. (*To himself.*) Sure, I could have lived with Claire for the rest of my life—we could have read the papers on opposite ends of the couch and slept in single beds. But I met Susan. (*Faint, inward smile.*) And we fell in love. As simple as that. (*Pause.*) Now it's over. You plan, you try to arrange the future, but you're cheated by circumstance. She went through hell for me and I can't even make it up to her. So nothing means very much, does it? You know, I feel a little like those people who come to your office to confess. I want to talk; I want somebody to listen. And when you're in this mood you need a priest—or a cop. (*Looks at* COLUMBO.) You're available. (COLUMBO *doesn't move for a moment; there is no sense of elation about him. Then he shrugs and holds open the door.* FLEMMING *goes into the reception room, pauses, turns back.*) You were always available, weren't you? (COLUMBO *is silent.* FLEMMING *looks at* MISS PETRIE.) Cancel all of my appointments, Miss Petrie. I'm going with the lieutenant.

MISS PETRIE. Yes, Doctor. (*The* TWO MEN *go out.* MISS PETRIE *looks after them, troubled. She opens her appointment book and pages through it, then dials a number. To phone.*) Mrs. Clark? This is Doctor Flemming's receptionist. I'm afraid we'll have to cancel your appointment this afternoon. . . . Why don't I call you back when I know his schedule? Fine, Mrs. Clark. 'Bye.

(*Hangs up, begins dialing another number. The door opens and* SUSAN HUDSON *comes quickly into the office.* MISS PETRIE, *startled, hangs up.*)

SUSAN. I'm sorry I'm late, Miss Petrie. Can the doctor still see me?

MISS PETRIE. But—I don't understand. We called your apartment and a man answered. He said there had been an accident.

SUSAN. Accident? What accident? (*Frowns.*) Something strange is going on. A policeman picked me up at my apartment. Then we drove around for a while and he just dropped me off a minute ago. (*Thinks for a moment, agitated, then starts for the office door.*) I want to see the doctor.

MISS PETRIE. He isn't here. He went out.

SUSAN. I'll wait for him.

MISS PETRIE. But—

(SUSAN *enters the office, stands for a moment indecisively.*

Then she sees the gift-wrapped box on the attaché case. She picks it up, sits down, and removes the white card. Pleased and surprised, she reads the inscription aloud.)

SUSAN. "To Susan: All my love, Roy." (*Touched by this she smiles, begins to open the gift.*)

CURTAIN

PROPERTY PLOT

ACT ONE, Scene 1

Dr. Flemming's Office
  Standing lamp
  Swivel chair
  Desk with phone, ash tray, cigarette lighter, cigarette box, prescription pad, pen and pencils, desk calendar
  Desk chair
  Bookcase/bar with book ("My Life In Art"), 2 bottles, 4 glasses
  Lamp
  Sofa
  Wall ledge—trade magazines
  Reception room chair
  Secretary chair
  Reception desk with phone with buzzer, appointment book, folders, pencils
  Chair Down Left

Off Left:

Flemming—Handkerchief, hat, coat, pen, address book, attaché case with dress and picture
Claire—Sunglasses, gloves, purse, airline tickets
Susan—Purse

ACT ONE, Scene 2

Dr. Flemming's Apartment
  Chair Right with hat and coat
  Chair Left
  Bar with lamp with 2 bottles, 4 glasses
  Ottoman
  Sofa
  Table with lamp, phone, phone list, ash tray, cigarette lighter, paperweight
  Writing desk with lamp, attaché case with dress, tickets, magnifying glass
  Desk chair

PROPERTY PLOT

Off Right:
2 suitcases, laundry bag, jewelry box with jewelry, gloves

Off Center:
SUSAN—Large purse with sunglasses, picture
Check, breakaway glass in window

ACT TWO, SCENE 1

DR. FLEMMING'S APARTMENT
  Chair Right
  Chair Left
  Bar with lamp with 2 bottles, 4 glasses
  Ottoman
  Sofa
  Table with lamp, phone, ash tray, cigarette lighter
  Writing desk with lamp, attaché case
  Desk chair

Off Right:
COLUMBO—Notebook, hat, coat, wallet and badge, cigar

Off Center:
FLEMMING—Hat, coat, pen, 2 suitcases

ACT TWO, SCENE 2

DR. FLEMMING'S OFFICE
  Standing lamp
  Swivel chair
  Desk with phone, cigarette lighter, cigarette box, desk calendar
  Desk chair
  Bookcase/bar with books, 2 bottles, 4 glasses
  Lamp
  Sofa
  Wall ledge
  Reception room chair
  Secretary chair
  Reception desk with phone

Off Left:
COLUMBO—(FLEMMING'S pen)

PROPERTY PLOT

ACT TWO, Scene 3

Dr. Flemming's Apartment
Chair Right
Chair Left
Bar with lamp with 2 bottles, 4 glasses
Ottoman
Sofa
Table with lamp, phone, address book
Writing desk with lamp, magnifying glass
Desk chair

Off Center:
Susan—Gloves, purse
Columbo—Key
Boy—Dress, laundry

ACT THREE, Scene 1

Dr. Flemming's Office
Standing lamp
Swivel chair
Desk with phone
Desk chair
Bookcase/bar with books, 2 bottles, 4 glasses
Lamp
Sofa
Wall ledge
Reception room chair
Secretary chair
Reception desk with phone

ACT THREE, Scene 2

Columbo's Office
Right wall clipboard
Chair
Coat tree
File cabinet
Table
Desk chair
Desk with phone, ash tray, sunglasses, desk lamp
Chair Right of desk

PROPERTY PLOT

ACT THREE, Scene 3

Dr. Flemming's Office
　Standing lamp
　Swivel chair
　Desk with phone, attaché case with package
　Desk chair
　Bookcase/bar
　Lamp
　Sofa
　Wall ledge
　Reception room chair
　Secretary chair
　Reception desk with phone

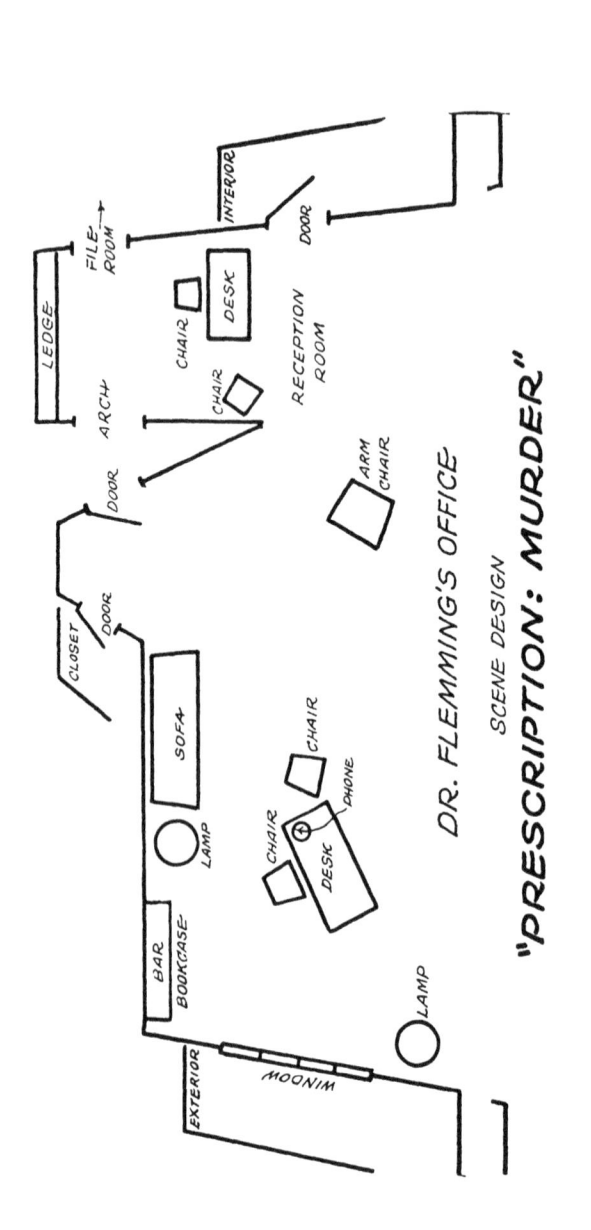

DR. FLEMMING'S OFFICE

SCENE DESIGN

"PRESCRIPTION: MURDER"

"PRESCRIPTION: MURDER"

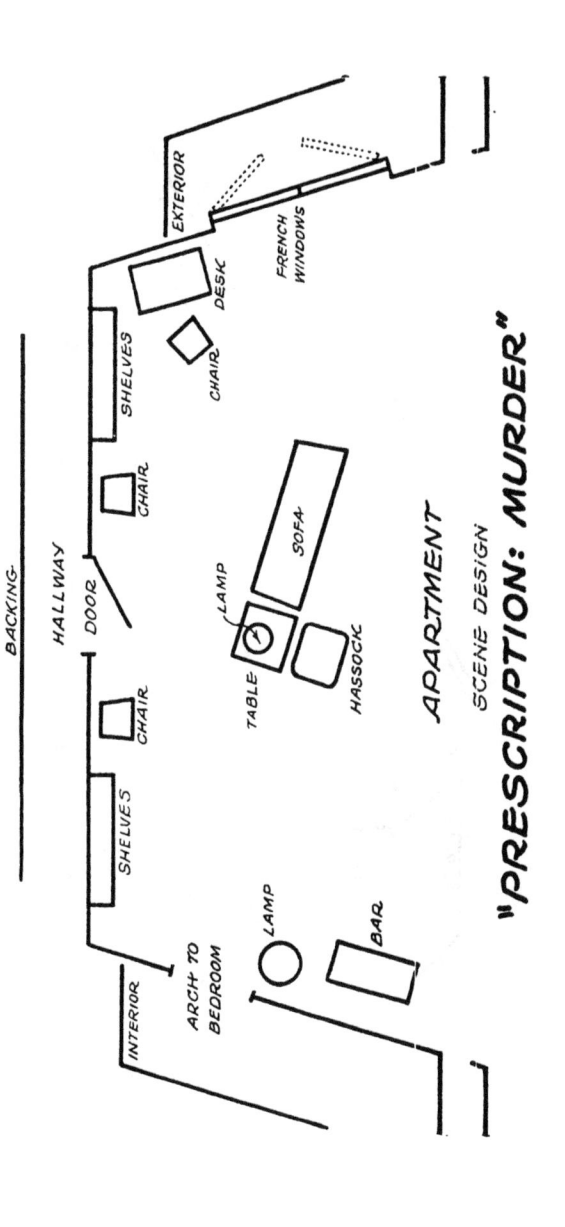

APARTMENT

SCENE DESIGN

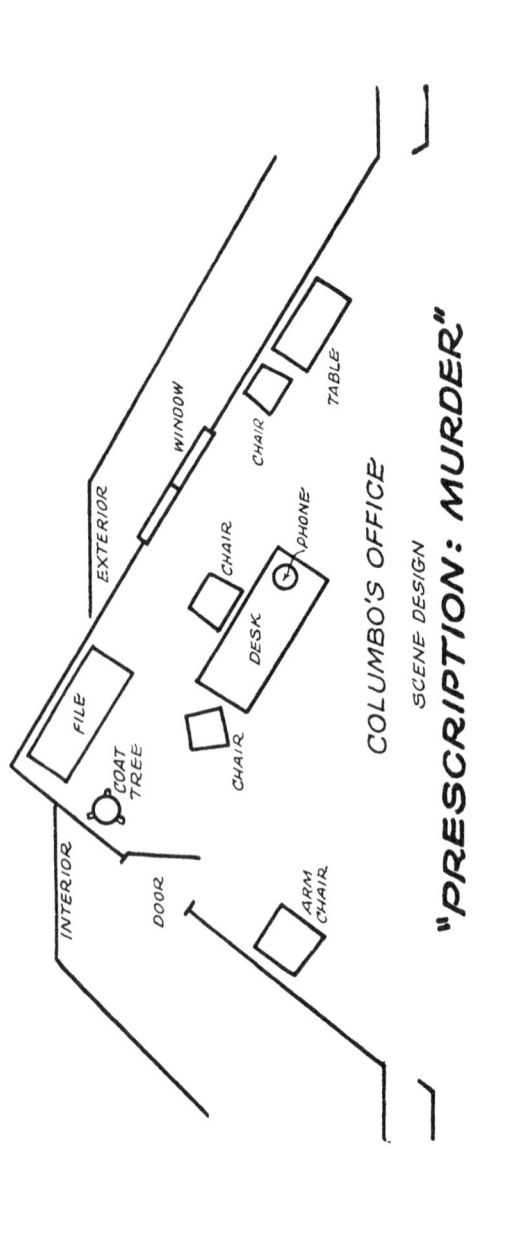

COLUMBO'S OFFICE

SCENE DESIGN

"PRESCRIPTION: MURDER"

WHITE BUFFALO
Don Zolidis

Drama / 3m, 2f (plus chorus)/ Unit Set

Based on actual events, WHITE BUFFALO tells the story of the miracle birth of a white buffalo calf on a small farm in southern Wisconsin. When Carol Gelling discovers that one of the buffalo on her farm is born white in color, she thinks nothing more of it than a curiosity. Soon, however, she learns that this is the fulfillment of an ancient prophecy believed by the Sioux to bring peace on earth and unity to all mankind. Her little farm is quickly overwhelmed with religious pilgrims, bringing her into contact with a culture and faith that is wholly unfamiliar to her. When a mysterious businessman offers to buy the calf for two million dollars, Carol is thrown into doubt about whether to profit from the religious beliefs of others or to keep true to a spirituality she knows nothing about.

SAMUELFRENCH.COM